THE LAST MACKENZIE
OF REDCASTLE

WITH COMMENTARY

The Last Mackenzie of Redcastle

by
Rosa Mackenzie Kettle

with an Commentary by
Alan McKenzie

Published by the Clan MacKenzie Society of Canada;
and the Clan Mackenzie Society of Scotland & the UK,
2015.

Originally published in London 1888 by James Weir

ISBN 978-0-9949628-0-5

First published 1888

Cover design and layout:
Duncan McKenzie
duncan@mkz.com

This edition published 2015
The Clan Mackenzie Society of Scotland and the UK
and
The Clan MacKenzie Society of Canada
580 Rebecca Street,
Oakville, Ontario Canada
L6K 3N9
alan@mkz.com

CONTENTS

INTRODUCTION

The Last Mackenzie of Redcastle is a history of the life of Captain Kenneth Mackenzie, eighth of Redcastle, written by his granddaughter, Rosa Mackenzie Kettle. She was a successful novelist, who brought all her novel-writing skills to bear when writing this account.

The original copy of this book, published in 1888 is an extremely rare volume. An Author's Edition was in the possession of Sandy Mackenzie of Dundee, the first president of the Clan Mackenzie Society of Scotland and the UK. He recommended that this historical romance should be reproduced because of its interest and rarity.

The proceeds from the sale of the book will be used as follows: fifty percent will go towards the maintenance of the grave of Sir Alexander Mackenzie in Avoch, Scotland. (Sir Alexander was the first man known to have crossed Canada by land.) The remaining fifty percent will be split equally between the Clan Mackenzie Society of Scotland and the U.K. and the Clan MacKenzie Society of Canada, a registered charity in Canada.

The book was edited by Alan McKenzie, the founding president of the Clan MacKenzie Society of Canada, and a life Lieutenant to Cabarfeidh (the Clan Chief, the Rt. Hon the Earl of Cromartie). The original text is preserved, except for the spelling of the name of one of the characters, Frazer. This was changed to Fraser, since he is supposed to be related to the Frasers of Lovat.

On researching Captain Kenneth Mackenzie, the subject of this work, it became very clear that this so-called history bore little resemblance to various other recorded histories of the man. For that reason Alan McKenzie has added a Commentary at the end of the book. The Commentary compares the wicked reputation of Kenneth taken from other sources to his apparently praiseworthy character in Rosa Mackenzie Kettle's book. The discrepancy becomes even more complicated when the histories themselves differ substantially from one another. In addition, Rosa changes the names of the main characters and dates in her book.

Because the Mackenzies of Redcastle have played an important role in the history of the Clan Mackenzie, Sandy and Alan thought it right that this book should be added to the growing number of volumes which detail the histories and power of the Clan Mackenzie in the Highlands over several centuries.

PART THE FIRST.

"Perish 'policy' and cunning,
    Perish all that fears the light,
Whether losing, whether winning,
    'Trust in God and do the right.'
Shun all forms of guilty passion,
    Fiends may look like angels bright;
Heed no custom, school or fashion –
    'Trust in God and do the right.'

"Some will hate thee, some will love thee.
    Some will flatter, some will slight;
Cease from man, and look above thee –
    'Trust in God and do the right.'
Simple rule and safest guiding—
    Inward peace and shining light—
Star upon our path abiding—
    'Trust in God and do the right.'

NORMAN MACLEOD.

CHAPTER I.

Not till the rushing winds forget to rave,
Is heaven's sweet smile reflected on the wave.

I shall make no apology for giving my hero the name of a great Highland family, since it belonged to him of right, and was his only heritage from a long line of ancestry.

More than one generation has passed away since young George Mackenzie looked sadly over the darkening Beauly Water from his hiding-place among the ancient woods.

His descendants possess only the plainly bound, much-worn Bible which accompanied him during his wanderings, his dinted sword, knee-buckles, and a small pair of pocket-pistols; the faded lines of his marriage-certificate in which may still be traced the name—which at present we shall not reveal—of his bride, and the signatures of her kindred; his seal, and a valuable diamond ring.

Nor do I consider myself bound to adhere strictly to truth in this romantic chronicle. Those circumstances which affect the principal characters are essentially true. In other cases names and dates have been purposely altered to prevent annoyance or misconstruction.

Many years have elapsed since that far-away time; so there is little cause to fear that this story of our grandfather will give pain to any mortal living, while the facts on which it is founded are well worth recording.

There is a point where the Redcastle woods come down to the margin of the loch where the beautiful, ill-fated, cruelly judged, enthusiastically loved Mary Stuart is said to have stood when she called the place—and it still retains the name she gave it—"Beaulieu," saying with a sigh, that the spot reminded her of "la belle France." Our own Queen has alluded, in the latter pages of her touching "Diary of Events in the Highlands," to the same scene, warmly expressing her admiration of its beauty.

The rose-hued ancient castle still overlooks the Beauly Water, with its terraced gardens, on which, since the epoch of our story, much wealth has been judiciously expended; - but there are no Mackenzies now at Redcastle.

"Muckle Colin," the big auld laird, sleeps with his ancestors; there let him rest in peace. Little is known of him except his name, some feats of sportsmanship, and a few facts respecting the management of his household which speak for themselves. Probably the indolent giant was more of an adept at tossing the caber, and striding over his own hunting-grounds, than in ruling his high-spirited second wife.

Our business lies with the only son of his first marriage; at whose feet the Beauly Water, in the grey of the gloaming, is gently rippling, while the wind, already higher up aloft and gradually rising, is singing a mournful dirge in the branches, which anon will toss wildly, rocking in the blast. As the breeze moans in the tree-tops, it seems to say, as it did when the hero of Charlotte Smith's quaint story, "The Old Manor House," bade adieu to his home, "Orlando will return no more;" a passage over which, in my earliest youth—it was the first romance which found entrance into our school-room—I invariably shed tears.

There was no moisture now in the young Highlander's eyes—only burning, fiery indignation, which had dried up the passionate drops that had sprung to them at first, brought there by angry mortification. He had been grossly insulted by the lady who occupied his own dead mother's place at the head of his father's table, in the presence of a numerous company of guests, who stood too much in awe of her temper to interfere.

His father, the big, lazy Highland laird, had not rebuked his wife, had not said a word in his son's behalf. George had risen and left that usually-hospitable board, with a rash unspoken oath on his lips, never to take the place which of right belonged to him beside it again.

No one but himself knew what the youth had borne, and borne bravely, before this last blow fell—one, perhaps, not heavier than many previous ones, but it is the last straw that breaks the back of the usually patient, pathetically moaning, over-weighted beast of burden of the desert.

Though scarcely conscious of bodily suffering, the poor lad was by this time half-starved. Neither "bite nor sup" had passed his lips since the scarcely touched dinner of the previous day, when each morsel seemed to choke him; and he had rushed away from the well-spread board to hide his wrath and grief in the woods.

He would have been as thankful now as the poorest crofter's child on his father's estate, of late indolently ruled, if anyone had put "a piece" into his hand; and full many a clansman would gladly have divided his own homely meal, or shared that of his offspring, with the Laird's son. But he had complained to no one—had not asked for help—had not realized his own condition and pressing wants.

He had not taken the trouble to stop and drink of the spring gushing out from a rock in the woods which was free to all, or even stopped to gather the freshly springing young cresses that grew beside the water-course, as he had done many a time when belated on some sporting expedition, hungry as a hunter, and easily satisfied with the simple fare Nature provides for her straying children.

He had wandered on aimlessly for a long time; and, when worn out with fatigue, he had thrown himself down to sleep in a hut in the forest piled with logs. There he had passed the night, unfed, ill-clothed for such exposure to the keen air of the Highlands; dressed, as he was wont to be, in his national garb, with only the addition to what he had worn at the dinner-table of his Highland cap and plaid, which he had snatched up as he hurried through the hall.

But he had slept, in spite of all discomforts, not heeding them; not even conscious of the want of accustomed food and warmth. He was very young, though past the age when runaway boys are apt to return to, as hastily as they have quitted, the paternal roof, after a very brief trial of the thorny paths of life. His wrongs, too, were deep and real. He had borne them long, but could not endure them longer. Yet he shrank from baring his wounds to the cruel scathing light of day—from bringing to light what he felt would make the clansmen cry shame on his father.

Not a crofter would have refused him bed and board, but how could he ask for either without betraying the Laird's culpable weakness? Better to die a hunted outcast in the woods or on the bleak hillside, where the foxes had their holes—the rabbits their warm cosy burrows—the birds of the air their nests, year by year, in the old trees to which they were flocking, noisily twittering and chaffing with each other as they flitted from bough to bough, or swooped in the gathering darkness close past his heated brow. They knew that a storm was impending.

Up and down beside the Beauly Water, listening to the flapping reeds, the rising wind, the waves lashing the pebbles, the youth slowly paced hour after hour. From this spot—he knew it well, and had sought it on that account—a glimpse of the light-red sandstone castle was visible catching the evening sunlight.

Its towers and turrets, high-peaked roofs, and pointed architecture, half French, half Scotch, glittered and gleamed in the level sunrays. One corner of the terraced garden, where figures were moving, could be seen, and he drew back among the trees. But there was no danger of recognition. The distance was too great, even if anyone in his father's house cared to look out for, or heeded what had befallen him.

A fiery gleam shot from dark clouds full of storm in the west, and a low growl of distant thunder travelled from hill to hill, foreboding a night of tempestuous gloom. Where could he take shelter and find food and rest? Where could he lay his aching, weary head?

The sound of the pipes, of martial music, The Gathering of the Clan, stirred the young man's blood. It came across the water from a lonely little inn, a clachan, hidden by the woods, where a party of soldiers with a sergeant were, he knew, beating up the country for recruits in the war-time. The strain ceased abruptly. Later on a church-bell rang out for a few minutes. The youth doffed his bonnet reverentially. Then all was still.

Though quite determined not to re-enter the Castle unless solicited, and assured of proper treatment as the eldest, indeed only son of the Laird, the thought of passing another night in the woods, fireless, supper-less, friendless—of the long hours of chilly darkness and the yet colder grey dawn and early morning—sent a thrill through the youth's frame.

Involuntarily there flitted before his dizzy eyes visions of the interior of the Castle—glowing wood fires, sparkling lights reflected from antique mirrors, burnished carvings, picture-frames and panels. Strains of music, softer than the bagpipes, rang in his ears—plaintive notes, wailing regrets, in which lay thoughts for the absent—sung by one, who not akin to him in blood, loved him as a sister; and the merry laugh of her boyish brother mingled with the wash of the water at his feet, and the rush of the wind in the tree-tops and among the branches.

He had just reached the point where in the solitude and darkness he might have given way to tears, when a little hand stole into his, and a boyish arm was thrown across his shoulder as he stooped to caress the young maiden.

"Hallo, old fellow! We've brought you some supper!" exclaimed a voice quite familiar and close to him. "Make haste and eat it. And here's your tinder-box and an end or two of candle and a warm rug. Didn't Morag greet last night, when I said how cold you must be! When are you coming home, Geordie?"

"Never!" said the youth firmly, as he warmly returned their greetings. "How did you contrive to find me?"

"Oh, we guessed that you would make your lair in the woods. It's warmer than the open moor or the hillside," said the boy. "But it's plaguy dark even now. I'd not like to stay here my lane much later. It's going to be an awful night. Did you hear the thunder growling behind the Black Mountain? We must not stay long. What can we do for you?"

The young girl clung to Mackenzie's arm, but she did not speak. She had stolen away from her mother's drawing-room in her simple white evening dress. Her hair, long and soft, was snooded with a pale blue riband, and a plaid, hastily thrown over her head and gathered round her, screened her neck and arms. In her girdle was a bunch of white heather, which George took from her, and, after tenderly kissing it, placed it in his bosom, saying:

"Give me this, Morag, as an omen of good fortune. It is our badge, too, and a pledge of faith and love. Donald, have you a coin or two about you? You will find my purse in the old cabinet on my table. It contains also my mother's picture and some old letters. Take care of them for me, and repay yourself. If there is anything left, give it to the old folk among the hills next winter."

The boy unbuckled his sporran, and emptied its contents into George's hand. There was a sprinkling of gold, some silver, and a heap of coppers.

"Mind, I won't have a bawbee of it back again, George. I'm glad my birthday was last week, and I have been nowhere to spend what your father gave me. But what are you thinking about? You're surely not ganging awa', like Prince Charlie, never to see bonnie Scotland again?"

"I don't know—time will show," said Mackenzie.

"Meanwhile, thanks, Donald, for furnishing the sinews of war or commerce, or travelling wherever fate may call me. Good-night, my dear brother and sister, for as such I shall always regard you. Dinna forget."

"That will we never do," said Donald heartily, wringing his hand. "It's more likely that you'll forget us if you go over the seas and far away."

Morag put up her white face and kissed her tenderly-loved adopted brother.

"I can't believe you are going really to leave us," she said, tearfully. "We shall come every evening, at the gloaming, and bring what we can. I'm sorry it is but little. Give me the basket, that is more likely to be missed than the scones and pasty. Here's your Bible, dear good George; I thought you'd miss it. Good-bye—God bless you!"

The lips fervently pressed, the delicate hands so fondly clasped, grew cold under the pressure ere they were reluctantly released.

A nearer roll of thunder gave timely warning. Before the storm broke the boy and girl were safe within the Castle walls, but all night long the lightning flashed and the rain came down in torrents over the woods.

More than one blasted trunk and scathed crown of foliage bore down the memory of that tempest: and the night was remembered long when the young heir, homeless and destitute, with the black clouds of heaven for his canopy and the wind singing dismally his lullaby, wandered among his father's woods or lay on the rough logs

in the forester's hut, scarcely sheltered from the impetu-
ous beating of the wind and rain.

CHAPTER II.

"Arise and go,
    For, in the ruddy west,
The sun sinks low; -
    And this is not your rest.

"Arise and go,
    The curlew seeks his nest
With pipings low;-
    And this is not your rest

"Arise and go,
    Rough places may arrest
Your steps so faint and slow;-
    For this is not your rest."

SONGS OF ERSKINELAND

The storm had cleared the sky, and all the clouds had vanished, when after a disturbed, comfortless night, George Mackenzie looked out from the log hut which had afforded him imperfect shelter. It was the bugle-call—the soldiers' *reveillé*–heard across the Beauly Water, which awakened him. He never forgot that summons to active life and duty.

He went to the spring and drank, as a mountaineer knows how to drink, the water gushing from the living rock. Then he held his head under the fall, and let it flow over his face and through his curly hair, performing such ablutions as circumstances allowed, before he opened his Bible which Morag had brought him. Presently a plunge in the loch would refresh him, and do away with the feverish fatigue caused by the agitation of the previous day and restless night.

The girl had rightly guessed that George would miss the Bible which had belonged to his mother, and since her death had been his constant companion and friend. He could not remember the time when he had not read at least a few verses, before the work or pastime of the day began.

He had been his mother's darling, and she was a gentle, God-fearing woman, who had been taken away early from the rough pathway which had been patiently trodden by the side of "Muckle Colin." While she lived, he had been a better man; they had prayed side by side in the church. Under the shadow of its walls, in ground consecrated centuries before, when it lay in ruins, she lay at rest. George often went there, at first trying to keep up with the giant's stride, but of late, alone. It was a long time since big Colin's shadow had fallen across the grassy hillocks and head-stones of that churchyard.

The passage in the Scriptures which attracted the youth's attention involuntarily this morning, was the wonderful account of Jacob's journey, when the Angels of God went with him. In that lone place beside the spring, with the first sunbeams glinting through the wet branches, gilding the leaves of the trees and sparkling in the water, he fancied he could see rainbows of promise, as well as ladders leading from earth to heaven.

He remembered that in the night, while he lay listening to the thunder, and watching through the openings in the logs, the fierce play of the lightning, the words sprung to his lips, "How dreadful is this place. . . . The Gate of Heaven!" Now all terrors of the night were over, and he thanked God heartily for the preservation of his young life, of which once more he felt the value. With boyish energy, after his simple prayers were said, he pushed and rolled together some of the great stones lying about until he had raised a cairn.

Some day, he thought, I may come here again; and then, if I am master, I will have a tower or perhaps a little church on this spot.

He worked on again with a will until the sun was high in the heavens, and the heat oppressive. Then he finished the small stock of provisions which his young friends had brought him, and lay down to rest for a while in the shade.

Very soon he was fast asleep; and he dreamt that he was a soldier coming back, sorely wounded, to his native land. Probably it was the pain caused by the scratches and wounds inflicted by the sharp edges of the big stones, which made him fancy that he had left one arm in some famous battle-field. However that might be, he was a hero, and Morag met him and put a laurel-wreath on his head; and gave him a capital venison-pasty, which they sat down to eat together under the trees.

The last part of his dream no doubt arose from his feeling very hungry. When he woke, the sun was declining, and there was no Morag at hand and no venison-pasty. He drank some water and ate some of the cresses with some scraps of bread which had fallen on the ground in the morning. Now he sought diligently for every morsel. If the boy and girl failed to keep tryst, matters would go hard with him. Still he hoped that the great Father who feeds the young lions and ravens would not forget him.

The chill hours of darkness were drawing near before he heard voices calling him, and saw Morag's white frock between the fir-stems. She looked pale and frightened, saying that one of the servants had followed them, but they had manged to slip away and hide themselves in the wood. They were afraid he was a spy, and that they would not be allowed to come out by themselves another evening. What would George do for his supper?

"God will provide," Mackenzie said firmly. "Do not trouble about me. This way of living, anyhow, cannot last much longer. Have you brought me anything to eat?"

"Aye, aye," said the boy, unfastening his wallet, and handing him a goodly supply; "we brought all we could, fearing lest we might not be able to come to-morrow. George, had you not better come home?"

"Has my father asked for me?" said Mackenzie anxiously. "I don't want to grieve him—does he show any signs of missing me?"

Donald hesitated. Morag, with instinctive womanly tenderness, exclaimed:

"He never took his eyes off your chair at breakfast and dinner. Oh, George, he must miss you, but he never says much. The dogs were all whining and sniffing about when I went with him to the kennels, and he gave such a big sigh—it quite blew the heads off some dandelions I was holding in my hand, intending to see what o'clock it was. I should have had to give two or three puffs, but he sent all the seeds flying at once. I said, 'The hounds are missing poor Georgie,' and he squeezed my hand till he hurt me, but he did not say anything."

"Then I shall not return," said George gravely. "Not until I am invited there will I take my place at his table again, to be sent away from my rightful place like a child or a whipped hound. I dare say the dogs miss me, and the pony. Morag, you will be good to them for my sake."

"Yes, surely," said the girl softly. "I will take care of all your pets and work in your garden, and never—never forget you any more than if you were our real brother. Donald, why don't you say as I do, that we will never forget Georgie?"

"There's no need for me to say it: boys don't talk so much as girls, but they remember longer," said Donald, severely. "I dare say the Laird is minding about Georgie, though he does not make such a clatter about it as you do. Is there anything more we can bring you, old fellow, if we get the chance?"

"No, no, don't get yourselves into trouble;" said Mackenzie. "Besides, I don't want anyone to know where I am, except yourselves. Most likely, too, before another night darkens over the woods I shall be far away."

"Well, you'll write and tell us what you are doing," said Donald; who had such faith in George's strength and cleverness that he scarcely realized how forlorn were his prospects.

"I'd not half mind running away from home and joining you when you've made your fortune, or helping you to win it. Be sure to let me know as soon as you've settled to anything. Redcastle will be a beastly place without you!"

"Oh, you would not both be so cruel as to leave me!" said Morag, bursting into tears. "It's breaking my heart to part with Georgie. If you go too I shall not have a sole to speak to about him, or ever hear what has become of him."

"Stay and take care of your sister, Donald, at all events for the present," said Mackenzie with affected gaiety.

"When I have made my fortune I will send for you both to share it."

He kissed Morag's white forehead and wrung the boy's hand, then, without another word, he plunged into the depths of the woodland. The girl stood as if spell-bound, watching him till he was quite hidden from view, then, taking her brother's hand, she went back, still weeping, with him to the castle.

Though the moon shone brightly over wood and water all through that lovely summer night, Mackenzie had even less sleep than during the tempest. In vain he tried to rest, gathering around him the warm rug Donald had brought; slumber was far from his eyelids. He was quite sure that their mother would not allow Morag and her brother to visit him again in his lair in the forest. Watchful eyes, spiteful tongues would spy out and report all their movements; countless annoyances would be heaped on himself when his hiding-place was discovered.

Just as he was at last dropping off to sleep in the grey dawn of morning, a strain of distant music and the sound of the church bell roused him completely; and he gave up all attempts to court repose. Wrapped in his plaid, with the rug strapped neatly together, George walked down to the lake shore. Perhaps as the drowsy world seemed for some reason or other to be astir he might find a boat and get a passage across the loch.

When he stood on the bank the cause of the disturbance among the village community was plainly manifest. A red glow of fire was rising above the woods; and in Highland villages composed principally of thatch-roofed cottages, there was always considerable danger of a conflagration soon spreading far and wide.

Doubtless the soldiers had been summoned to assist; the music he had heard was the note calling upon them to assemble. Mackenzie walked with the light, long swinging step of a Highlander round the end of a loch and soon came to the point of the danger.

A party of soldiers, obeying military orders with alacrity, were stripping off the roofs of some cottages closely adjoining those that were blazing. A sergeant stood in the middle of the street giving orders, which were promptly obeyed.

When Mackenzie offered his assistance, the old non-commissioned officer looked at him from head to foot; admiring his tall, stalwart frame, and thinking, even in the hurry of the moment, what an admiral recruit he would make if he were disposed to take service.

"Aye, aye, by all means. Help like yours is not to be despised. Make room there!" he called out to the men, and in a moment Mackenzie was in the line of active workers. He was not recognised, for the moon had sunk, and the dawn was breaking dimly through mist. The village, too, was some distance from the castle, and no one expected to see him there, alone and on foot, at that hour between night and early morning, when news travels most slowly.

He obeyed orders, and did his part so well that when danger was over the sergeant thanked him warmly; adding that he wished he had a good many such fine fellows in the regiment.

George accepted his invitation to enter the Clachan, and wash the smoke out of his throat with a glass of whisky; but he took sparingly of the liquor. He asked some questions about the regiment, which had been recently raised in the Highlands. Finally he signified his readiness to try the fortune of war, accepted the King's shilling, and walked out of the Clachan a private in the - ~ Regiment of Scottish Infantry.

One half-wild look around, one sigh for the past, and Richard was himself again; ready to take advice, to obey orders, to bear hardships and privations. Unprovided for the life that lay before him, save by his loyal heart and trust in Providence, his dauntless courage, high spirits, honest intentions, and unswerving principles.

He took nothing with him when he marched away from the vicinity of his father's castle except his mother's Bible, the rug, and some of the coins Donald had given him, his plaid, and the clothes he stood in, which were speedily exchanged for the ordinary uniform of a private soldier. Nothing else except the bunch of white heath, the Mackenzie badge, which he had taken from Morag's belt and treasured next to his heart.

CHAPTER III.

"Hugged in the clinging billow's clasp,
    From sea-weed fringe to mountain heather,
The British oak with rooted grasp,
    Her slender handful holds together,-
With cliffs of white and bowers of green,
    And ocean narrowing to caress her,
And hills and threaded streams between:-
    Our little Mother Isle, - God bless her!

"His home! The Western giant smiles;
    And twirls the spotty globe to find it;-
This little speck the British Isles?
    'Tis but a freckle—never mind it!
He laughs till all his prairies roll,
    Each gurgling cataract roars and chuckles,
And ridges stretch from Pole to Pole,
    Heave till they crack their iron knuckles."

OLIVER WENDELL HOLMES.

The young Highlander bore patiently the many morti-
fications which he encountered at first in his career
of duty after joining the depot of the regiment in which
he had enlisted. He soon became a favourite, and was respected by both officers and men.

Strict obedience to discipline, smartness of appearance,
spirit and gentleness, were combined with readiness to

oblige a comrade, and respectful bearing to his superiors in military rank. These qualities, prompt intelligence, and remarkable good looks, soon gained him notice and approbation also in high quarters.

Very speedily he obtained marks of favour, and before long the stripes, which denoted his rise in the ranks. In all exercises and in every routine of life in barracks he associated on friendly terms with his comrades, gaining their regard and good opinion. Only in their recreations he never felt disposed to take part. At that time more especially, the diversions of the British soldier were not to his taste, nor did he ever profess good fellowship in them; but at those hours of freedom it was a relief to find the barrack-room empty, or perhaps only occupied by one or two quiet spirits, and to be able to read, and study his profession undisturbed by noisy uproar.

One thing he never omitted, and that was to read some portion of the Bible which Morag had brought under her plaid to him in the woods by the loch-side. The book seemed like a legacy from his mother, and he valued it highly. Neither did he neglect to pray night and morning. At first his comrades jeered and scoffed; but they soon found that, good-humoured as he was about trifles, in serious matters Mackenzie was not to be trifled with. They left him alone after the first or second day. In time some of them imitated him.

On Sundays, after church, to which he was marched off with the rest, he would often take his Bible, and go and sit by the sea shore during his hours of liberty; some-times reading, sometimes thinking—as he listened to the incoming or outgoing of the tide—of the ripple of the Beauly Water on the pebbles of the loch-shore, and the sound of the wind in the tree-tops among his father's woods.

He never breathed a word which betrayed his origin; yet all his comrades knew that he must have been born and brought up as a gentleman. Some of the officers questioned him, but he declined to answer or evaded their inquiries. He had borne the yoke in his youth, was still bearing it, and knew how to hold his peace and keep silent.

When he had gained his three stripes, which he did as soon as possible, though he had more responsibilities he was freed from constant intercourse with his inferiors, and advanced to another, much higher grade of military experience; but he still remained unpretending, and very considerate for those who now ranked beneath him.

When the regiment was inspected previous to leaving England, the General noticed his alertness favourably, and after the review he received orders to present himself to the old officer. George would have shrunk from the ordeal if possible, for he had recognised in the hero of many fights a frequent visitor at Redcastle; but no excuse would serve for declining the flattering command.

He could only hope, as the veteran had given no sign of recognition, that he might as a mere boy in his father's house, among a number of sportsmen, have entirely escaped notice. A deep flush mounted to his fair forehead as he stood respectfully, keeping in the shadow, at the entrance of the large room to which he was ushered.

"So, you young scapegrace!—we have run you to earth at last!" exclaimed the General the moment the door was closed, not heeding Mackenzie's military salute, but coming forward hastily to meet him; while the abrupt greeting dispelled all hope that the famous old foxhunter's eyes were not as keen as they had been on the Leicestershire wolds and the Ross-shire moors. "Oddly enough, I was the first person to whom your father wrote when the fact that you had enlisted came to his knowledge. Did you think that I should not know my old friend's son? You have not got his bulk, 'tis true, but you bid fair for Muckle Colin's inches; and you are the very image of your mother—as sweet a lady—a Highland lady—as ever walked the earth.

The General bowed his grey head in reverence; and shook hands cordially with the handsome living representative of his dead friend.

Mackenzie's eyes were full of tears; for a moment he could not speak.

"Well, I shall try not to ask any questions you may not like to answer; or, if I do, I will excuse you for not replying to them," said the old officer kindly. "It's an ill bird that fouls its nest; and I fear, my boy, yours was made to cramp your young pinions sorely. Why did you not come to me, or to any old friend of your family, in the first instance? It would have saved a world of trouble. But that cannot be helped now. Tell me at once, without my questioning you, as much or as little as you like about your home troubles."

In a few terse sentences George put such a picture before the veteran hero that the hot blood mounted to his cheek. He did not utter a word of blame respecting his father, but the fact that he had suffered his only son to be so insulted spoke volumes.

The General took two or three turns about the room before his anger cooled down; then he said:

"Enough, my boy, more than enough, has been revealed to justify your flight; though I still regret that you did not appeal to your father's—or, better still, to your mother's friends. But all shall be set right. I hear that you have been studying your profession diligently in every leisure moment. Neither has your time been ill spent in learning to perform thoroughly the duties of those who are—even now that, through your own merit, you are a non-commissioned officer—your subordinates."

The General took another turn, and then added, laying his hand kindly on the youth's shoulder:

"It is well to learn to obey; and it is also good for a man who is in command to understand thoroughly, practically, the work of those under his orders. Now you must be restored to your fitting grade in society. Be patient, and remember—'All's well that ends well.'"

George withdrew after taking a respectful leave of his father's and his mother's friend.

The General did not forget him. Many individual marks of kindness reached him, smoothing his path and brightening his arduous career. As soon as the inevitable delay in all matters permitted, he found himself gazetted as an ensign in the 60th Foot, and ordered to join his regiment immediately, then in active service in the Colonies.

He was sorry to leave the Highlanders, and not a man exhibited a sign of envy or jealousy. His advancement was felt to be his due. The first time when he crossed the parade-ground and saw his old comrades in turn, as he passed their posts, lift their hands to their caps to salute him as an officer, Mackenzie was the only person who felt embarrassed, almost reluctant.

"We'll meet again, sir, on the other side of the Herring Pond," said the sergeant from whom he had taken his first lesson in drill, and who had handed him the King's shilling in the Highland inn. "I knew from the moment I saw you fall into line at the fire, that you were a gentleman's son, and from the way you obeyed orders and handled the buckets that you'd make a rare soldier! And now I'm right glad, and so are all the men, to see you in the right place at last, and on your way to distinction."

When, later on, George took leave of his former companions, after giving them a farewell supper, long and hearty were the cheers which concluded the simple banquet, which was very orderly and yet genial. Many a time in after life, when his path crossed the honourable line followed by the ⸺ Highlanders, a familiar sentence, a cordial greeting, was exchanged between the young officer and the men with and from whom he had learnt the first hard lessons of a soldier's career. He always had a tender feeling for that noble regiment.

The Royal American, as it was at first called, afterwards the 60th Rifles or Shropshire Regiment, to which he was appointed, had carried their colours on many a field of glory before, as they have done since, that time. Their colonel was another old friend of George's family, and had enjoyed many a good day's sport on the Ross-shire moors.

Mackenzie soon learnt his new duties, which seemed mere child's play compared to those which he had performed with uncomplaining assiduity. As the General prophesied, he found then and afterwards that the time spent in the ranks was by no means thrown away.

There was a spice of romance in what was known of his career, which recommended him to the fancy of the ladies, whilst his manliness speedily made him at home among gentlemen; but he did not lose his heart to any fair one, or waste much time in amusement. Morag's bunch of white heath was the only gift from a girl's hand which he treasured; the earnest study of his profession most ardently prosecuted.

He was glad when the time for embarkation arrived—

when life and a manly career opened before him; and it was with the high heart within him pure from vice and full of generous enthusiasm, that Mackenzie set sail for the New World.

CHAPTER IV.

There's music in the wild cascade,
    There's love among the trees;
There's beauty in the banks and braes
    And balm upon the breeze;
There's a' of nature and of art,
    That maistly weel could be,
And oh, my love, when thou art there,
    There's bliss in store for me.

Then meet me, love, by a' unseen
    Beside you mossy den;
Oh, meet me, love, at dewy eve,
    In Morag's fairy glen.

"Was that song written for you, or were you named after it?" whispered a young officer as he stood close beside Muckle Colin's step-daughter, and with courtly assiduity handed her across the drawing-room at Redcastle after she had with some trepidation finished her performance.

"No; it is an old ballad, not written for me. Morag is a family name in my mother's house," said the young girl in an equally low tone, for she felt that her mother's eyes were upon her.

Those words always reminded her of the gloaming,

years ago, when she and Donald had bid a last farwell to her dear heart's brother in the woods. In her hazel eyes there was a passionate glow, and tears glistened in her long lashes.

"I was certain those words had even deeper meaning for you than for others," persisted the young Highlander— a kinsman of young Fraser of Lovat, who was paying a farewell visit to his kindred before joining his regiment in America. "In those dark woods we visited to-day there must be many a fairy glen fit for lovers' tryst."

"Yes, the woods on Beauly banks are very bonny," said Morag timidly. "But, oh, they—they are so lonely! If you had left one you loved dearly to sleep under their canopy, with the lightning for his taper and thunder for his lull-aby, you would shudder at them even on the brightest summer-day."

"I have heard of that parting, and I have seen a sprig of white heather like your shoulder-knot—the Mackenzie badge—among a soldier's treasures," said Captain Fraser, bending his tall form until his lips almost touched the tender blossoms fastening the girl's scarf and guarded by a pin fashioned out of a ptarmigan's claw.

"I had noticed the owner of that badge, and I could have sworn that he was a gentleman, as many of the privates in our Hieland regiments are. But there was something more than is common even among the gentry about him. One day I came upon him when he was sitting on the river-bank in an English valley. It was the Sabbath, and he had his Bible open before him, with a sprig of white heath lying on the page he was reading. I marked how reverently he lifted it aside to read the words underneath. Neither the gesture nor his hands were those of a common soldier, and I challenged him at once to deny that by birth we were equals. He could not tell a lie, though he would not agree to it. We sat by the river together for an hour, and talked about Scotland. But he would not tell me his name, and in the service he bore another."

Morag listened to him with breathless attention.

"Long afterwards, when, through the interest of his mother's friends, he had obtained a commission in our regiment, which was just on the point of sailing for America to teach the saucy colonists better manners, I heard Mackenzie's story, and guessed that he was the quiet yet stalwart youth with whom I had foregathered by the English river. Since then we have been constant and intimate companions. We shall meet again ere long. Will you not entrust me with a token or message?"

"Tell him that I and Donald weary for him sadly. That we love him better than ever. And, oh, bid him take care of himself for our sakes," said the girl, looking straight in his face, her eyes full of unshed tears; "I am afraid that the lesson you are trying to teach the rebels is one difficult to learn and hard to practise; if the news-sheets we sometimes see may be trusted, these malcontents are enemies not to be despised."

"Oh, they are coming to their senses—they must see, or they will see, that they can do nothing without British soldiers, disciplined troops, to protect them against those Indian raids which are more terrible than civilized warfare. Depend upon it, the struggle will soon be at an end."

Morag sighed. "I hope you are right, but I must not stay talking with you longer. My mother, I see, wishes me to come to her. Oh, if I could send a little token, a few lines of writing to George, I would be forever grateful," she added, in a hurried whisper.

"Bring it to Morag's Fairy Glen to-morrow, at the gloaming," Fraser replied in as low a tone. "The place at which you looked back sorrowfully when we were riding with your father."

The girl did not speak, but Lovat Fraser read acquiescence in her smile as she hastily left his side.

The buoyant heart of the young Highlander was in no way cast down by dread of any perils which might await him at the hands of the "Provincials," as they were contemptuously called, and their army. Like most of the Loyalists of the day, especially military critics, he thoroughly despised the new patriotic levies.

Little did the arrogant young officer anticipate the bloody day on Saratoga heights when his gallant kinsman, Fraser of Lovat, instead of winning back his father's forfeited coronet would fall victim to the patriotic fury of the insurgents, like a torrent coming down in flood-time from the hills.

The man on the iron-grey horse rallied the line in vain—even the dreaded Hessians, the men about whom women frightened their children, broke and fled before Benedict Arnold's terrible charge; as he rode down upon them, mounted on the powerful black charger, named after the patriotic, much-beloved leader, Warren, who fell at Bunker's Hill.

The man whom Gates pronounced to be capable of any rash act, sent officer after officer vainly to recall him to the subordinate position assigned to him, saw the moment when history would crown his country's cause, and led her sons on to do or die. Such men seize or make opportunities, careless what may be the consequences to themselves of their heroic impulses.

But we must not anticipate ⸺. As yet the fortune of the day was undecided. News came tardily from the distant seat of war, and was often converted into shapes differing widely from the reality. Fraser had all the prejudices of his castle to contend with before his naturally ingenuous nature and generous impulses would prompt him to do justice to a nation which, after struggling against grievous wrong, had unsheathed reluctantly the sword but had now thrown away the scabbard.

His heart beat as he passed under the boughs of the woodland and heard mingling with the flow of the burn, the rustling of the leaves, and the love song of the birds in the thicket, a voice, which was often to ring in his ears in the heat of battle, singing sweetly a verse of the ballad to which he had listened the night before at Redcastle:

"Come when the sun in robes of gold
    Sinks o'er yon hills to rest,
And fragrance floating in the breeze
    Comes frae the blinding West;
And I will pu' a garland gay
    To deck thy brow sae fair;
For mony a woodbine-covered glade
    An' sweet wildflowers are there."

Lovat could not help joining in the refrain which followed each verse of the song—

"Then come, my love, by a' unseen
    To Morag's fairy glen."

His enthusiasm was somewhat damped on hearing a rather rough manly voice chime in; and, the next moment, Morag's brother, auburn-haired Donald, came out of the woodcutter's hut to meet him.

"Oh, come in, come in, Lovat," he exclaimed heartily; "Morag was afraid of the darkness and asked me to keep her company through the woods. I was glad enough to come with her when she told me you could talk to us about George. He is our step-father's son, though not our mother's, and our hearts are often sorely wearying after him. So you really saw him trailing a pike in the ranks— or whatever it is the common soldiers do there! Anyhow I am sure he did it well. There never was such a fine fellow!"

"Yes; he does all things well. He got all his stripes for good conduct, and was a universal favourite," said Fraser, trying to get over his bitter disappointment. "But, Donald, don't you think that two of the family are more likely to be missed than one from the gay company in the drawing-room? Had you not better go back now? I will see your sister safely home. To-morrow we will stroll over the hills and talk about George."

"What do you say to that, Morag?" said her brother. "You asked me to come, and I'm not going to desert my post—unless "– he added in a lower tone—"you wish it?"

"No, no," said his sister, blushing deeply. "Let us keep together."

Captain Fraser turned away, mortified; but he paused when she said quietly:

"Wait, I have not given you my packet for George."

The young soldier bent low to receive her commands, taking from her hand, which trembled as he touched it, a small square white packet, tied across with a blue riband. He ventured slightly to press those quivering fingers.

"Tell George, our dear adopted brother," the girl said, in an agitated voice—"that he is not—that he never will be, forgotten as long as we remain at Redcastle; and that we all long for his return—his father, I am certain, most of all. He seldom goes out now, but sits moping over the fire like an old man, even in the summer weather when the woods he used to love are green and fair; saying that the evil days are come—that luck has left the auld house since Geordie was awa'!"

Her voice broke; Donald exclaimed impatiently:

"Why do you say we shall not forget him as long as we remain at Redcastle? Is there any chance of our flitting? Even if there were—if we went to prison or to the end of the wide world, as he has done, we'd remember Geordie!"

"Of course we should," said his sister, reproachfully. "You might—you must—know, Donald, that was not my meaning. But I am afraid the Laird is right, and that evil times are coming—are near at hand. I think that George ought to come back. There are people coming and going, marking the trees, counting the plate and linen, and the books in the library. Oh, Donald, you know as well as I do, that our mother does not love the old place, does not care for George's rights. I dared not say this in my letter, but will you tell him, Captain Fraser, that when this perilous war is over, - and, oh, I trust it may not last longer than you expect—he is sorely wanted at home again."

Lovat promised to do her bidding faithfully. He had seen and heard enough, while staying in the neighbourhood among his own kindred, to prove that Morag's were not idle fears. The Laird's strength was failing fast. Muckle Colin was not the man he had been either in mind or body. His clever wife could turn him round her finger, and keep him fastened, beside his own chimney-corner, to the string of her embroidered apron. The young heir's rights were not safe in their keeping.

Donald did not prove a troublesome guardian. Perhaps the hearts of his young companions spoke more plainly in his inattentive presence than might have been the case when they were alone. The voices of the wild birds coming to his ears as they settled themselves to rest among the trees in that solitary place, the rush of the cataracts in the dell, the stealthy tread of some night-loving animal in the thicket, told him more than the whispered talk of the lovers to which he bent no ear.

Though her brother, true to his promise, kept close to her, it was on Lovat's arm that Morag leant, when the darkness increased and the path grew rougher with the roots of the old trees stretching across it.

Without the embarrassment which often attends a *tête-à-tête*, they felt themselves alone together in spirit among the slumbering woods. The star-bespangled skies shone through the forest boughs upon two happy trustful faces. Morag's lashes did not shut out the heaven that lay behind them.

Their talk was often about George, but it returned sometimes to themselves, or wandered on to the future when Lovat, peace being restored, hoped to come back to Scotland crowned with glory. He tried to win encouragement to the hope he entertained that in company with her beloved, adopted brother, a welcome would await him at Redcastle.

Neither of them liked to allude to changes which might, ere long, enable George to rescind his proud resolution not to tread these halls again. Nor did they distinctly allude to any alteration in the ruling powers in that ancient Highland home. But in the loyal heart of Morag, as well as Donald, the heir's rights were sacred, and they longed to see him restored to his befitting place.

Muckle Colin might rouse himself from his stupor and summon his son to his side. A thousand things might happen to bring matters round and right all wrongs. Nothing seemed impossible to their youthful imaginations quickened by love. Nothing except that the two gallant officers, now so full of life and hope, might be stretched on some dreary battlefield in the far west, immovable; as many and many a brave man was lying at the moment when they were spinning webs of love and glory, bespangled by the moon's rays as she rose above the Beauly woods and Ross-shire hills.

Morag started when she saw those silvery beams stealing athwart an open glade in the woodland.

"Oh, how late it is! How long we have been away!" she exclaimed breathlessly. "I hope we shall not be missed from the drawing room."

Donald reassured her, saying that time passed pleasantly when people were well amused, as the guests at the Castle were sure to be at that hour. They could hear the sound of music from the house through the open window, merry voices and laughter.

He advised his sister to step in quietly at a side window, and change her dress which was wet with dew, while he and Lovat went boldly in at the front door. No one would question them as to their proceedings. There was no time for parleying, only one lingering pressure of the hand which, rested on his arm, before Lovat released it.

Their final parting, for he was to depart early the next morning, was formal enough under the stern glance of the Lady of the Castle. No one but themselves and Donald knew of the precious packet for the wandering heir, or of the unwritten messages which were to be delivered on the other side of the Atlantic.

Nor did anyone guess, as the young officer bent low, according to the fashion of the day, before the pale young maiden at her haughty parent's side, that their real farewell had been sighed rather than spoken under the stars in the Beauly woods.

PART THE SECOND

"In earth's broad temple—where we stand,
    Fanned by the eastern gales that brought us;
We hold the missal in our hand
    Bright with the lines our Mother taught us;
Where'er its blazoned page betrays
    The glistening links of guilded fetters,
Behold the half-turned leaf displays
    Her rubric stained in crimson letters.

"Beneath each swinging forest bough
    Some arm as stout in death reposes;
From wave-washed foot to heaven-kissed brow
    Her valour's life-blood runs in roses;
Nay, let our brethren of the West
    Write smiling in their florid pages
One half her soil has walked the rest
    In poets, heroes, martyrs, sages!

"Enough! To speed a parting friend
    'Tis vain enough to speak and listen,-
Yet stay—these feeble accents blend
    With rays of light from eyes that glisten.
Good-bye! once more—and kindly tell
    In words of peace the young world's story—
And say, besides—we love too well
    Our Mother's soil—our Father's glory."

                              OLIVER WENDELL HOLMES.

CHAPTER V.

That sunshine had a heavenly glow
    Which faded with those good old days;
When winter came with deeper snow
    And summer with a softer haze.

It is far from our intention and beyond our power to give a detailed account of the great struggle for American independence, which followed that December night, when the cargo of the tea-ships was poured out unsparingly into Boston Harbour; and later on, the pealing of the great bell at Philadelphia in the warm air of July, gave token that Pennsylvania and Maryland had agreed to join in the declaration of freedom.

A mighty concourse was assembled under the black walnuts, which are said to have been stately well-grown trees, when Penn carried out the plan made out under the Buckingham-shire beeches, and founded on the bank of the broad Delaware, a stately city; which he resolved should resemble "a fair green English country town with houses set in gardens." Fruit trees, hazel, hawthorn, and white walnut, of which he brought the seeds from England, blossomed beside the ways crowded by multitudes of people.

That solemn manifestation of a people's will was then and there pronounced, which when it speaks with power must not be disregarded; - and it is still remembered, and solemnly yet joyously kept in every corner of the inhabited globe to which the sons and daughters of those Western Colonists have penetrated. There are not many regions left unvisited by Americans. An eloquent writer of their own says:

"The sons and daughters of those rebellious Colonists, have kept that day with sober thankfulness, with rowdy merriment, with exultant pride, with solemn memories, from the forests of Maine, to the swamps and jungles of Louisiana, and from the Atlantic to the Pacific Oceans. As that day comes round, it is remembered on the other side of the world—in the nooks of the Alban Hills, in passes of the Apennines, among the Umbrian mountains, and by the banks of Arno; in many a German town, in the heartless streets of Paris, and in ships tossing in mid-ocean, far from any land. Even amidst the eternal desolation of the north, in the brief Arctic summer, that day has been celebrated. On that day every American, wherever he may be, thinks of home, and if he be in a far country, feels the pangs of home-sickness.

"If it happen to him to keep that day in the mother-country, whose rule his ancestors threw off, he can perhaps afford after the lapse of a hundred years, to remember it with some abatement of the old bitterness, even though with no less of the old pride. There are wounds that ache for centuries. Time itself but skins them over—and this is one. But, after a hundred years, the inheritor of that day can perhaps afford to remember, that his blood, his language, his stubborn independence itself, are all English."

That beautiful city, planned by the English Puritan who refused to bend the knee to the Royalty he and his forefathers acknowledged and faithfully served, might surely own the tie without a blush! Even free-born citizens might be proud of a common origin with the son of the gallant old Admiral, whose enormous debt to a bankrupt Monarch was acquitted after the restoration of the Stuarts, by the gift to his heir of a tract of land in the Western Wilderness; totally uncultivated and unprofitable until, redeemed by lavish care from barrenness, it was made by the great English settler in the West to blossom as the rose.

Mighty as that state now is, when William Penn and his companion, Pearson, first landed the country was devoid of all trace of civilization. Chester Creek—so named in memory of his native city by Penn's faithful friend—the first place they stayed their course at, ran up into a wilderness, beautiful, but uncultured, stretching from the Alleghenies to the river Ohio, and northwards to Lake Erie, tenanted only by a few Dutch and Swedish settlers, and traversed by tribes of wandering Indians.

Those free-born Englishmen, who prized personal freedom, liberty of thought and speech better than home and fortune, rank and luxury—who had left their much-loved country most reluctantly, and still in exile loved her dearly—were worthy ancestors to look back upon and imitate, alike in the surrender of all that their hearts held most dear and in their faithful remembrance of the past.

Let us pause for the moment while the other bells of the good city of Philadelphia are taking up the tone and ringing out joyfully over the declaration of independence, and look back at that solemn yet simple treaty to which "Yea" was the only answer on both sides made by the white and the red men at the Place of Kings, under an old gigantic elm-tree, which had canopied many a gathering of the Sachems.

William Penn, then in the very prime and vigour of manhood, with no outward pretence of sanctity, but with the love of Christ and of all mankind warming his noble heart, has the chief place of honour. Dressed in ample garments, slashed and buttoned, with flowing auburn curls hanging on his shoulders, drooping cavalier's hat, lacking only the feather, - ruffles, and cuffs fine and white, as his biographers describe him—he was, as one who then beheld him says, "The handsomest, best, and liveliest gentleman ever seen."

Penn was no cavalier against innocent recreation. He often astonished the natives in conference by starting up and joining in their games, excelling the best among them in feats of skill and activity; and he allowed his family to witness their festivals and dances. But he never forgot, or let them think he had forgotten, the Great Spirit, Who, as he taught them, rules alike and impartially over all His children.

He told them that "Onas," the one Great God, Who reigned in that heaven to which good men go after death—Who had made them and Himself out of nothing, and knew the secrets and the hearts of white men and black—knew that he and his people wished to live in peace, wronging no man, serving them all fairly in every way, meeting the red man in the broad path of uprightness and good will.

He wished that all roads should be free and open as well as the doors of the white men's houses and the lodges of the red-skins. That the children of Onas and the Lenni Lanapè should listen to no false reports, but they should run and tell each other of any threatened danger to either party. If any wrong were done they were not to right themselves but to complain to the chief and to Onas, that justice might be obtained through the verdict of twelve honest men on either hand; and the wrong be buried in a bottomless pit.

This bond of good fellowship he trusted might endure as long as water ran down the creeks and rivers, and the sun, moon, and stars kept their courses.

Neither oath nor seal were required. Penn stood under the great elm in that verdant council-chamber. Tamanent, the good old chief Sachem, long remembered and revered, held in his hand the chaplet of peace, which always made the place where it was used and all present inviolable. The governor laid the treaty on the ground, the Sachems agreed to respect it, and it was kept.

As soon as the mother-country roused herself to believe in the fact, as in many more recent cases too long ignored, that the Provincials—as the rebellious colonists were called—had in serious earnest cast off the yoke which had been galling beyond endurance, great exertions were set on foot to restore order and tranquility. Several Highland regiments were sent out, and the Indians flocked from all quarters to see the strangers, whom they at first regarded as brothers from their similarity of dress, declaring them to be of the same race as themselves.

During the war, however, all ornamental appendages were laid aside, the English officers only wearing a narrow edge of gold lace round the borders of their jackets. All glitter was discarded, for the Indians, after the idea of brotherhood had been abandoned, aimed chiefly at the leaders, whose uniforms and dauntless intrepidity made them fatally conspicuous.

The experience gained by our hero whilst serving in the ranks and as a non-commissioned officer was not thrown away when he became a commander of men, whose trials and troubles were known to him. George Mackenzie also possessed the chief characteristics of a Highlander. He was brave, ardent and faithful, as well as zealous; while his somewhat peculiar training and the sorrows of his youth had checked his natural impetuosity and taught him to control his temper.

After the war ended it is recorded in the annals of the time that applications were made by the inhabitants of districts in Ireland where Highlanders had been quartered that these regiments should be sent again to the same stations. Many Irishmen had volunteered to join their ranks and fought, as is their wont, well.

Mackenzie soon gained the confidence of his men, each one feeling himself known and understood, his difficulties taken into account, and his efforts and exertions promptly recognised. Among his brother officers he was popular; and his superiors acknowledged his ability to conduct and readiness to undertake hazardous enterprises, which he carried out with prudence and discretion, beyond what might from his age have been expected.

His regiment, though not composed of the Highlanders whom he would fain have led, was associated with them on many occasions, and he found or made friends among their officers. But his own messmate, Lovat Fraser, who had lately seen his home, Morag, and Donald, was his most constant and intimate friend and companion.

They were both thorough soldiers to the manner born; and as neither of them had frittered away their energies in dissipation or idle loiterings in garrison towns and country quarters, they had still the full bloom of youth, with its crown of beauty on their fair northern faces and abundant brown locks. Their talk was principally of foughten fields, past, present, or to come; and of manly sports in their Highland glens or on the mountain side, where they had stalked the deer and heard the cock-grouse welcome the dawn. They also had many theories, some perhaps Utopian, concerning the conditions of the soldier and the peasant in every land under the sun. On all topics they conversed freely; sometimes by the camp watch-fires, at others in their respective tents, whenever duty allowed them to hold friendly counsel together in those stirring times.

Since the surrender of Burgoyne's army, after the bloody battle on Bemis Heights, the British officers had learnt to treat the Provincials with more respect; and to confess, though they never admitted the possibility of failure, that the foe they had to contend with was worthy of their arms.

Morag's letter had been safely delivered, read, and re-read not only by her adopted brother, but by his friend its faithful deliverer. Fraser loved to linger over one page, which simply as it was worded, had cost the girl more trouble than all the rest of her tender, thoughtful communications. It ran as follows:

"These home-tidings will be brought to you by a young officer who is going out to rejoin his regiment, and he says that you are always *bons camarades*. I think he will win himself a name in history, as he has done in the Strath, for he has been first in all the games. He has the lightest foot in the dance, and Donald says it is as fleet and untiring on the heather. My mother does not look upon him favourably, but he has won everybody else's goodwill. Even your poor father, who is but too apt to see through her eyes, bade him 'God speed ye!' heartily. I am sure he longed to send you, too, his blessing. Many wept sorely at parting, for he goes to danger, perhaps to death, as you too, dear brother of my soul, have done. I am afraid those rebels are more terrible foes than your letters make them out to be, and I tremble when I read in the public prints about the Red men in their war-paint stealing out from their trackless haunts. May the good God keep you both from harm!"

It might be only womanly tenderness mingling with sister-like affection which breathed in those words, which Morag certainly had not intended for his inspection; but Fraser's heart beat as he read them. The last rays of twilight, the glimmer of twinkling stars coming out in the gloaming over Morag's fairy glen, seemed to shine on the page as the brothers-in-arms read the letter among the haunts of the rebel leader, Marion—the Swamp Fox—on the banks of the Savannah River.

CHAPTER VI.

"Our band is few—both tried and true—
  Our leader frank and bold;
The foeman trembles in his camp
  When Marion's name is told.
Our fortress is the good greenwood,
  Our tent the cypress tree;
We know the forest round us
  As seamen know the sea.
We know its walls of thorny vine,
  Its glades of reedy grass,
Its safe and silent Islands
  Within the deep morass."

BRIANT

Francis Marion, the famous Guerilla leader in the struggle for American independence, who perhaps contributed more to the success of the cause than any man except Washington, was, like that great general, exemplarily single-minded; his whole life expressed the most unbending fixedness of purpose.

No longer young, grave and reserved, devoted to the performance of military duty, without ostentation or visible yearning after glory, he yet felt his heart burn within him when he was released from dull garrison duty in the new barracks which then occupied the site of the present

College at Charleston, and ordered on active service, to take the command on Sullivan's Island.

Marion's Brigade sprang into existence during the darkest days of the revolutionary contest. It was composed of men who were born to contend with the elements, and to take advantage of every accident of wind and weather, swamp and flood. Now here, now there, travelling as if borne on the wings of the wind, through pathless forests and quaking bogs, the Swamp-Fox, as their daring leader was called, never failed to surprise the regular soldiery. In their pursuit of game and of wild beasts they had become familiar with their daily and nightly haunts; and their own hardy habits as hunters made them insensible to fatigue or hardship.

Clad in homespun garments, without an ounce of superfluous flesh on their lank, sinewy frames, these men glided between the tree-trunks, following a trail like the Indians, knowing every wild bird's call, and able to imitate the weird cry of the crane, and the hoarse scream of the vulture or raven. They had no fears of the solitudes haunted by alligators on the river's bank, where the waters flowed through dismal swamps; they shrank not at the monster's roar. Safe in their profound knowledge of the secrets of wild nature, they had well-nigh learned to rule over her.

Although the fall of Charleston had let loose Tarleton, the cruel warrior whose name inspired terror, Marion and his brave band swept the country fearlessly. Guided by unerring instinct more than by military skill, disdaining the tactics of ordinary civilized warfare; avoiding danger, for his numbers were few, and never disregarding the indications of its approach, the wary leader never failed to read the lesson of caution which even a bent twig or a trampled sod of turf might supply. Drawing back when the enemy was prepared for resistance, and falling upon his victims the moment fancied security led them to indulge carelessly in the luxury of rest by some moonlit stream, when the Guerillas were supposed to be far away, Marion inspired his foes with superstitious dread.

A panic fell upon the bravest when, suddenly startled from slumber, they beheld him, mounted on the noble steed captured at Black Mungo Swamp, towering above them; his silver crescent reflecting the moonbeams, relieved against his dark leather cap, gleaming as brightly as his black, expressive eyes. Both crescent and cap were said to have belonged to a British officer, the former having been his gorget. On it had been inscribed the words, "Liberty or Death."

When Colonel Tarleton, dashing rider as he was—for he had followed the fox over the Leicestershire wolds, and dyke and ditch, fearlessly—came to the edge of Ox Swamp, and saw the tangled wild vines hanging over the pathless bog, he is said to have drawn in his rein sharply, saying:

"Come, my boys, let us go back. We shall find the Gamecock" (meaning Sumpter): "but as for this old Fox, the devil himself could not catch him!"

"Woe to the luckless soldiery,
      Who little think us near,
On them shall burst at midnight
      A strange and sudden fear:
When starting from their sleep in dread
      They snatch their arms in vain,
And those who stand to meet us
      Are beat to earth again;
And those who fly in terror deem
      A mighty host behind,
And hear the tramp of thousands
      Upon the hollow wind."

After all, these sounds, like the tread of trampling multitudes, might come from the skeleton trees and gigantic reeds when the winds were let loose over the blasted forests and swamps and howled above the waste. The tread of a few horsemen, mingling with these unearthly shrieks and rushing rustling murmurs, might easily be taken for the *avant courriers* of an immense host.

Then sweet the hour that brings relief
      From battle and from toil;
We count the battle over,
      And share the battle's spoil;
The woodland rings with laugh and shout
      As if a hunt were up,
And woodland flowers are gathered
      To crown the soldier's cup.
With merry song we mock the wind
      That in the pine-top grieves;
And slumber long and sweetly
      On beds of oaken leaves.

Grave men there are by broad Santee,
      Grave men with hoary hairs,
Their thoughts are all with Marion
      For Marion are their prayers!

And loveliest ladies greet our band
   With kindliest welcoming,
With smiles like those of summer,
   And tears like those of spring;
For them we lift our trusty swords,
   And lay them down no more
Until we have driven the invader
   For ever from our shore.

This daring leader of a dauntless band could control his own passions, and exercised unbounded sway over his followers. Though still lame, in consequence of a leap from a high window, when the doors were locked to prevent him quitting the room where one of the two convivial gatherings, which were the fashion of the day, was being held, Marion appeared to be ubiquitous. The rumour of his gallant exploits flew before him, as though the quivering reeds and ghastly piles of driftwood through which the wind swept, rattling the dead branches, told the tale to each other.

CHAPTER VII.

Fair and green is the marsh in June,
Wide and warm in the sunny noon,
Flowering rushes fringe the pool
With slender shadows, dim and cool;
From the low bushes "Bob White" calls,
Into his nest a rose-leaf falls,
The blue-flag fades; and through the heat,
Far off, the sea's faint pulses beat.

George Mackenzie, now a captain in His Majesty's service, and his friend Major Fraser, were out on reconnoitering duty among the rich lowlands near the Savannah River.

Not far off, later on in the annals of that bloody war, in which brother fought against brother, friend against friend, a battle was fought, in the front of which, more than once, men locked in the fierce death struggle, looked into each others faces with a start, recognising features once dear and familiar.

At present the scene was peaceful enough. Where the white tents of the royal army were to be pitched under the hanging wood, the leaves rustled in the light wind; and were reflected in the clear stream welling through interstices in the white coralline wall of rock which crossed the wide valley, and underneath which flowed the main body of water.

Little did the two young officers think that a thousand stand of British arms would one day choke up that pellucid spring, and that the clear waters of the Creek would run red with blood; nor that the swamp-fighters of the Bush, opposed for the first time in pitched battle to the flower of the British army, would hold their own and carry off the chief honours of the day; their leader, Francis Marion, the Swamp-Fox, receiving the thanks of Congress for his services on that well-fought, hotly-contested field.

Nothing more terrible than hunger and exposure, unsheltered, to the miasma which creeps at nightfall over the marsh-lands, now threatened the two friends as they stood talking together about their native land. George remembered the nights spent in the Beauly woods in his boyhood; since then he had learnt many a hard lesson of endurance. It was, however, advisable to reach some place where food and shelter might be obtained for themselves and their jaded steeds, which their soldier servants were leading along gently at a short distance.

"Marion and his swamp-fighters are luckily not close at hand," said Fraser. "If our reconnaissances are correct, they have swept down to the Pedee, where it is hoped Watson and Digby will soon give an account of the fellows. What a wilderness this is—and, I suspect, where it does not want beauty—most unhealthy. I wish we could find four walls and a roof to shelter us."

"Let us mount and ride on," said George, "anything is better than inaction. Suppose we trust to the instinct of our horses? Our own senses seem at fault.

No sooner said than done, and, after a time, matters appeared to improve. There were large patches of culti-vated soil—the forest receded—the marshy land was dried up, the waters finding a bed in the broad river which tra-versed the level meads of Savannah.

There was as yet, however, no indication of any place where entertainment for man or beast could be obtained. The tired horses could not much longer keep up the pace which had brought them far away from the lonely creek.

Mackenzie and Fraser dismounted again, and gave the reins to their followers, whose sturdier steeds were also showing signs of exhaustion.

The shades of evening were falling rapidly, for in that southern clime day departs suddenly, when a change be-came observable. Trees not natural to the soil grew beside the way, and a better made road showed that care had been taken to facilitate travelling.

At a bend in the stately river's course the woods opened, having evidently been cleared away to afford a prospect of the beautiful stream; on which the rising moon was now casting a broad band of light, and shin-ing on the walls of a white house standing on an emi-nence near, but out of reach, even in flood-time, of the water.

A long white wall enclosed small fields and huts, with cultivated gardens round each low habitation, and crops of maize. At the sound of horse hoofs numerous dogs came out barking vehemently, but they retreated obediently at a summons from within. Lights passing from window to window betokened watchfulness, perhaps alarm; for the situation chosen for what appeared to be a little colony was very lonely, and the time was one of the greatest insecurity.

It was out of the question to pass by, and lose the only prospect which had presented itself for miles and miles, of rest and shelter for the night. Bidding their attendants keep a little in the rear, but within call, the two officers approached the residence guarded by the white wall.

The lowing of cattle, as well as the barking of dogs, was heard plainly within the enclosure, but they encountered no hostility. Even the mastiffs showed only friendly marks of attention. The dwellers in the wilderness, now thoroughly aroused, would, it might be hoped, be equally well disposed.

There were several doors in the long wall which enclosed a spacious corral, where in times of especial danger the animals could take exercise. Over the principial residence a sort of watch-box had been erected, for the purpose, no doubt, of surveying the country and scanning any intruders.

It was an immense relief when the two young men approached the gate, to hear themselves courteously greeted in English, and to find that their claims as weary, be-nighted travellers, at once acknowledged, and food and shelter for the night promised for themselves and their weary horses and attendants.

The whole party were at once admitted without appar-ent precaution, and their horses led off to the compound. No questions were asked, although those were times when gentlemen's houses were strictly guarded, and weary trav-ellers were often refused admission unless some guarantee was given that their intentions were not hostile.

But the old family servant, with his powdered hair, and faultlessly neat costume, seemed in no degree intimidated. The young officers found every necessary comfort in the two rooms adjoining each other, which were appropriated as guest chambers, and always kept in readiness for chance visitors. The strangers' rooms they were usually called.

After removing as much as possible all signs of travel from their garb and persons, Fraser and Mackenzie fol-lowed the servant who had waited upon them along mat-ted passages to a cool, wide verandah, where they were received by the Master and Mistress of this hospitable dwelling, and whence they were soon marshalled in order to a room where the table was lavishly spread for a late dinner or supper.

The Chevalier, or, as he preferred to be called, Doctor Lucena, was a healthy-looking, clear complexioned man, somewhat reddened and perhaps a little rougher than when he first pitched his tent in the wilderness. Manners formed in a high courtly circle after a learned career at the University still further improved by foreign travel, had acquired more ease and possibly less of the polished formality of the day, since he had embarked in agricultural pursuits and given himself up to the love of out-door nature and its study in the new world.

Not so Madame! Delicately beautiful, with the fine features and colouring of some of those old miniatures which have descended to us, as her's has done, from our maternal ancestors; Madame Lucena was still *grande Dame*—looking as if the wind had never been suffered to blow rudely upon her.

Their manner to each other, and to their unexpected visitors, possessed the very pink and flower of courtesy. Perfectly at their ease, and free from self-consciousness, they at once made the weary travellers feel at home. The repast hastily replenished proved amply sufficient and eminently satisfactory. The various dishes, composed of the best materials the country could produce, were all particularly well-cooked and admirably served. The old servant seemed to feel a peculiar pleasure in handing them round, and seeing them fully appreciated.

It was rather disappointing to the young officers that their agreeable host and hostess seemed to have neither sons nor daughters. Like clings to like; and beautiful as Madame still undoubtedly was, nothing fairer could be desired, something a trifle younger would have brightened their home.

Even this want was unexpectedly supplied. Before dinner was half over, a violent knocking commenced behind the panels of the banqueting-room. Madame looked at her husband and smiled.

"Surely there is no need to keep our girls cooped up," she said, "in that prison-like cupboard? These gentlemen are friends," she added in a still more cordial tone— "British officers—Loyalists. There is nothing to fear. Sometimes we have guests of quite a different stamp, from whom it is well to hide our brightest jewels. All are received at Casa Bianca."

The knocking had by this time become furious. Fraser and Mackenzie could not resist the inclination to liberate the concealed damsels. The panel gave way when the Chevalier touched the spring, and, amid much laughter and some confusion, two young girls were released from their dismal durance. As the lights the young men had snatched from the table flashed into the recess, they lit up the dark eyes, already shining with innocent smiles, of Rozay Morais and Clara Lucena, the latter the only daughter of the house, the former its youngest and gayest ornament.

No need to say that the conclusion of the repast was much merrier than its commencement, although the girls declared that it was the unusual hilarity of the feast which had roused their indignation at being excluded. What could be the use of their being immured in darkness when light and joy were on the other side of a thin partition, behind which they dared not even talk to each other in whispers?

Though they were not English they spoke the language fluently. The Doctor having spent several years in England, and taken his degree at one of our seats of learning, his family had become familiar with the habits and customs of the country.

Rozay Morais, though her eyes were dark hazel, had an exquisitely fair complexion and auburn hair. Through its thick waves a riband was passed coquettishly, almost in the Scottish fashion. Many a maiden by Beauly Water wore the snood in the same way.

Her cousin was taller, darker, and graver, though at the present moment she was laughing gaily. They loved each other like sisters, and had never been parted since the time when Rozay as an infant had been staying in her Guardian Uncle's house, when political troubles in Portugal obliged him to quit Lisbon hurriedly and fly first to England, ultimately to America, taking his orphan niece and his own wife and daughter with him.

Information had reached the Chevalier from a sure source that he was supposed to be implicated in the conspiracy of the Marquis de Tavora, which had nearly cost the King his life; and, although the accusation was false, it imperilled his liberty. There was no time to send Rozay home, so she shared the banishment of her relatives and became the adopted child of those who loved her as well as their own dark-eyed daughter.

Accident placed George and Rozay together at their first meeting. He studied her tastes, and persuaded her to make up for lost time in partaking of the delayed supper. She had a girl's healthy appetite, and readily followed her example, especially enjoying the delicious fruits fostered by that southern clime and rich soil; but she only touched with her rosy lips the glass in which he besought her to drink as a pledge of success to the Loyalist cause.

"Do not urge it. My girls have never tasted wine," said the Chevalier. "It is all very well when people are older, and may require the good gifts of God, but in youth stimulants are not needed. I am glad to see that, in spite of your fatigue, you are both so moderate; for in this warm latitude cooling drinks are most suitable and refreshing. Take another slice of melon or some bananas. How different they are here to the dry, tasteless importations known by the name in Europe!"

Madame rose from the table, and the gentlemen not wishing for more wine, followed the ladies to the wide veranda, which was the favourite gathering-place for the family in fine weather.

The moon was shining now with a brilliancy unknown in northern climes upon the wide river and its rich level meads. Tall reeds, like lances fringed the stream, their pointed heads gleaming as if barbed with steel. Flags waved like martial banners. The loud call of the frog, the softer murmur of innumerable insects filled the warm night-air, which was balmy and scented. In the darker spaces of the landscape, fire-flies were visible, darting across from stem to stem of the low bushes. All was serene and solitary in the plains below.

"It was from this spot that my wife and I watched the remarkable gathering of the clouds which was said to foretell the outbreak of the war," said the Chevalier. "It seemed indeed, as if armies were marshalled, and the dreadful boom of artillery splitting the skies asunder. Those who witnessed the spectacle from the mountain regions say it was still grander, but it was awful enough here. Wars and rumours of wars were then the common subjects of conversation, but the rebels had not crossed the Rubicon. We were alone here, anxious and dispirited, our girls at school."

He paused for a moment, and then went on:

"My wife shuddered and shrank back when I called her to stand by me and see the opening of the celestial contest, but the fascination was irresistible. Over the bend of the river, where the moon shines down so placidly, masses of lurid vapour had collected in a dark funnel-shaped column, from which volumes of smoke-like clouds rose upward and then floated solemnly away, following the course of the stream. Suddenly the heavy canopy overhead parted; portions of film, spectre-like, drifted across the sky. From the opposite side a host seemed to issue and meet them in the centre where the sky was luminous. Next came the crash of battle, lightning flashes, heavy groans of wind or distant thunder. Then all became wild confusion, as though the clouds of battle gathering over the scene interrupted our view. Soon afterwards came the news that war was actually declared."

"Would that it were ended!" said Rozay, who had drawn closer to her kind guardian. "We saw a strange gathering of the clouds before a great storm in the city, but it was not nearly so grand as your description. I wonder what sign there will be in heaven when peace is proclaimed."

> "The moon with its broken reflection
> And its shadows shall appear,
> As a symbol of love in Heaven,
> And its golden image here."

These lines, written much later, might have served as an answer to Rozay's question, only on Savannah's banks the reflection was not broken. It fell over land and water in a flood of golden radiance, and lit up the bright eyes and waving tresses of the girl as she leant upon the broad balustrade.

The Chevalier hurriedly drew the heavy curtains which protected the veranda.

"Go in Rozay. There is a light mist creeping up yonder, and though the night is balmy now it will bring a chill with it. See, it is gathering over the marsh, and will soon reach the river bank and be upon us. There will be no harbinger of peace to-night; more likely after the great heat a tempest."

The family retreated into the large room from which

the veranda, generally used as an apartment, opened, and where lights had been arranged. The girls had their instruments of music there, and soon discovered that the Highlanders could take part in glees and duets.

The evening passed pleasantly away, helped on its course by song and conversation. Not less pleasantly, perhaps even more delightfully, because in those stirring times there was so much insecurity as to what might happen on the morrow.

The gliding mists gathering over the banks and meads of Savannah were not more dangerous or more rapid than the stealthy march of wild bands of Guerillas or crafty savages, tribes of hostile Indians, which from time to time swept over the country.

Such placid home like Casa Bianca, often being left black and smouldering when the war-cloud which settled on them most often at that darkest hour before the dawn, which Indians choose for their approach, passed away in the morning, like smoke before the breeze.

CHAPTER VIII.

As Life's unending column pours,
  Two marshalled hosts are seen,
Two armies on the trampled shores
  That death flows back between.

One marches to the drum-beat's roll
  The wide-mouthed clarion's bray
And bears upon a crimson scroll
  "Our glory is to slay!"

One moves in silence by the stream,
  With sad, yet watchful eyes,
Calm as the patient planet's gleam
  That walks the clouded skies.

Along its front no sabres shine
  No blood-red pennons wave;
Its banners bear the simple line,
  "Our duty is to save."

The change which often comes after the full moon, set in that night; and on the morrow wild gusts of rain swept across the river, and the dry water-courses became beds of torrents.

So rapidly did the river rise, and so tempestuous was the weather, that it was dangerous to cross by the usual ford, and the bridge was many miles away. The Chevalier persuaded the young officers, who were not at all unwilling to postpone their departure, to remain another night; and rest themselves and their weary steeds in their pleasant quarters at Casa Bianca.

Their time was not altogether wasted; for few men in that distracted time and country possessed better means of obtaining information, or were so well qualified to make use of it, as the learned Doctor. The Indians regarded him with reverence, on account of his knowledge of the secrets of Nature and the healing powers of shrubs and plants. His skill as a physician, was regarded as miraculous; and they often brought sick and wounded warriors, or the ailing and feeble among their tribes, placing them without fear in what they called "The White Man's Sanctuary."

These red-skinned patients were always tenderly nursed by the ladies of the family, and treated with simple honest care by the Doctor. They were suffered to go free at once after recovery, even though sometimes suspicions of crime and wrong lay upon them; but they had trusted in his honour and it never failed them.

As long as they were under his roof nothing could exceed their patience, and their gratitude was undying. As long as life lasted, the life they deemed that he had prolonged, any members of the household of Casa Bianca might tread the paths through the swampy greensward in perfect security. The Indians kept watch over them; word was passed from man to man, to keep them safe from harm by night and by day.

In the white house, there was not a single offensive weapon, and only the most ordinary precautions were taken. Every traveller in need of rest and food was allowed to pause there on his way, and was supplied with all that he required, without a single question being asked. It had even happened, more than once, that hostile parties had been lodged at the same time within the compound, and had laid down their tired heads in peace on that blessed neutral ground.

Penn's "Holy Experiment" whether men of different races might dwell together under equal laws, in the faith of one Great Spirit, was here put in practice on a small scale, and so far, it had answered perfectly.

The young officers listened respectfully to the good Doctor's theories; though their military training inclined them to wish for a speedier end, for the present unnatural quarrel, than the slow spread of peace and good-will. They had not his wide experience, nor his great loving charity, which made him regard all men as brothers, equally need-ing allowance and forgiveness in the sight of the one all-perfect Father.

Within the white boundary-wall lived a happy commu-nity. Some were freed slaves, some preferred servitude under so kind a master; but provision was made, that at his death, all should be at liberty and so run no risk of passing under a more galling yoke.

With regard to the future prospects of the war now raging between the mother-country and her children, Dr Lucena reserved his opinion on many points; but he freely owned that he thought the high hopes entertained by the British officers of the speedy termination of the conflict were illusory. When men fought for independence, and women were ready to resign every comfort and luxury to aid them, the struggle was sure to last long and to be severe.

Nothing would satisfy the colonists now but their full recognition of what they held to be their rights. If England was to continue to be their mother, the children abroad and at home must share and share alike. On no other terms would they return to their allegiance.

From these arguments, in which the reasoning, however good it might be, did not convince the young warriors, Fraser and Mackenzie turned to the ladies of the family, with whom they soon became intimate. Madame Lucena, being less well acquainted with the English language, required the help of one of the girls to make herself quite intelligible; but it sometimes happened that appeals were made to them for assistance which were quite unnecessary.

Neither of these young maidens could remember the fearful earthquake which, three years after madame's marriage, laid low the principal square and palaces in the beautiful capital of Portugal; but its painful details were quite familiar to them from anecdotes told by their nurses in childhood, and by others who had witnessed that awful national calamity, as well as the Chevalier and his wife. Madame could scarcely bear even now to speak of it. The dark-eyed graver cousin took up the strain when her mother broke down in her first sentence, quite overpowered by agitation, and unable to find words with which to continue her narrative.

The women had carried the children out to the grand Plaza, where there was free space, just when the tremendous sea-wave which engulfed a great part of the city swept up to it. The falling of the church-towers, the wreck of palaces, the shrieks and wailings of the affrighted multitude, who thought that the great day of judgment had arrived, were terrific. Clara fancies she could recollect hearing them herself; but as she was an infant in her nurse's arms, her little brother only a year older, it was impossible that she could remember the awful scene.

Long afterwards the wealthiest nobles and citizens dwelt in tents and low, strongly-built tenements, as it was found that the more lofty and aspiring, and apparently substantial, the edifice might be, the more surely was it the mark for ruin.

"Madame will not tell you what was regarded as a miracle wrought by her loyal devotion," said Rozay, affectionately regarding her kind motherly friend. "I really think like Clara, I must have heard and seen it all, so vividly are the events of that awful day impressed upon my memory; but I was not born till some weeks afterwards. The scene

I am going to try to describe took place in one of the finest palaces in Lisbon, where my uncle and his family and madame's aunt, an old blind lady, resided. When the towers were falling, and the air was full of dust and mortar from the ruins, the servants rushed into the poor blind lady's room, entreating her to leave the dangerous shelter of those lofty, but already crumbling walls, but all was in vain. She was paralyzed by terror, and literally could not move.

"Another shock came, and the affrighted domestics fled; leaving with her only our gentle mother, as I love to call her, for she has been a mother to me. Madame had flown to her rescue on leaving the great church in the Plaza. The two helpless women clung to each other, in what they thought would be their last embrace—the blind lady close to the tottering wall, the one who could see beholding the dark threatening sky through the widening apertures where the great stones were parting.

"That side of the palace fell, but the opposite corner of the room where they stood remained uninjured. There was little more than standing space left, but they were safe. When the wall and parapet crashed down and the roof sank, that little coign of vantage stood firm; and those who came to search, weeping for the bodies of the two ladies found them unhurt, still locked in each other's arms. No wonder it was regarded as a miracle. It was one in reality—a miracle of faith, love, and loyalty, which crowned its heroine with a crown of sanctity thenceforth for ever!"

Madame drew the agitated girl, who had knelt down before her, nearer and kissed her fondly.

"That was not the only instance of fidelity and affection shown in those dreadful days," she said. "I never look at that carved set of shelves and the old china set upon them, all so fragile and precious, saved from the wreck of our palace, without remembering gratefully how by day and night our faithful black slaves, now our freed and faithful servants, searched the ruins to recover my husband's valuable title-deeds and my jewels, besides other articles of great value. Much of the property to which the deed related was ruined, but we escaped better than many others.

"I had worn my diamonds and part of a set of emeralds," Madame added, after a pause of emotion, "at a Court ball, the night before this terrible convulsion of nature. They were lost; but happily, the rest of the emeralds were in my jewel-case, which was found by our black servants and brought to me. Delicate vases of oriental porcelain were actually found unbroken, though much costly jewellery, ornaments, and plate were never recovered. There were nightly marauders about, and crimes, at which one shudders in looking back, were committed in the very face of those gloomy horrors.

"Ah, my children—my angels!" the poor lady exclaimed. "Let us not think or say more about that terrible time; or of the dark days of suspicion which followed, and made us exiles from our beautiful Lusitania. We are, thank

God! safe and happy here; but this is not our home. These western wilds can never be like our native land—our beautiful Lisbon palace—our Quinta on the banks of the Tagus."

Rozay took up her guitar and slung it on her graceful shoulders, anxious to dissipate her kind Aunt's melancholy reminiscences. Her voice was soft and tender as she sang a little American ballad, in which the wild charm of the forest seemed to lurk:

> The moon shines bright and her silvery light
>   Through the forest aisles is glancing;
> And with trembling beam in the rippling stream
>   A thousand stars are dancing.
> No sound is heard, save the lonely bird,
>   That hoots from its desert dwelling;
> Or the distant crash of some aged ash
>   Which the axe of time is felling.

Rozay's song had the desired effect, giving Madame time to regain her composure. The evening passed pleasantly; but Fraser, who admired her dark, beautiful cousin excessively—and might, perhaps, have been tempted to forget Morag if he had not suspected that her thoughts were pre-occupied—noticed that, ever and anon, when the wind rose louder, and the river rushed past with a hoarse roar, Clara trembled and grew suddenly pale.

After a while, as the tempest deepened, she rose quietly and went into the veranda, putting aside the curtains which had been drawn across the rough wooden shutters, for the openings were not glazed, even the curtains were seldom let down.

There were apertures in these rude defences, behind the drapery which shrouded her figure, and she gazed wistfully through them at the angry sky and swollen stream. Neither moon nor stars were visible, like the radiant lights in Rozay's forest song; all was gloomy and threatening. The girl's heart beat strongly as, in its inmost recesses, she prayed silently for one who might be—nay, probably would be, since love was his conductor—exposed that night to the fury of the storm.

CHAPTER IX.

"Never did the sun in the balmiest of climes rise with more brilliancy than on the memorable 1st of November, All Saints' Day, 1755. All nature seemed to rest in perfect confidence in the calm beauty of the serene and deep blue sky, and to repose in the stillness of the silent air. The proud palaces and lofty Churches of Lisbon were faithfully reflected in the broad bosom of the Tagus, whose crystal tide was unruffled by a single breath.

"Alas! in a few hours this smiling scene was to be exchanged for horror, misery, and desolation; and, as if the fiends of darkness suddenly released from bondage had plunged themselves precipitately on the doomed city bringing in their train earthquake, violence, rapine, murder and sacrilege, all things were marred; Nature ceasing to be beneficent, and Man to be human!"

"Memoirs of the Marquis of Pombal,"
BY THE CONDE DA CARNOTA.

"From the Monarch, our good King Jose, to the peasant, all looked to our great Minister," said Don Diego, when, the ladies not being present, the young men referred to the terrible time of the earthquake which he had witnessed.

"The Court was at Belem—all were in tears and utter dismay. 'What is to be done?' the King asked, looking round upon his helpless, trembling attendants; when Pombal, hastily summoned, appeared before him. His immediate reply was:

"'Bury the dead and feed the living.'

"What he said he did. Wherever he was most wanted there was that great man found. For days he lived in his carriage, whence hundreds of decrees were issued maintaining order, and providing for all the terrible exigencies of the moment. Often these mandates were written in pencil, and never copied, but they were unhesitatingly obeyed. We all thought him more than human; prejudice and jealousy were for a while silenced. The threatened pestilence was averted by obedience to his prompt measures. The wretches who took advantage of that awful visitation, and tried to violate the sanctity of unprotected private dwellings, were stopped at every door they assailed by armed guardians of life and property. Under his care the wretched weary citizens lay down without fear of violence in their ruined homes.

"For those whose houses were utterly wrecked, and who had only the canopy of the skies above them, Pombal provided temporary shelter. In addition to numberless cares to ward off danger, he took measures to prevent the landing of African pirates, hovering about the desolate coasts.

"It was my privilege at that time to possess a large share of his confidence. I might even venture to call myself his intimate friend," said the Chevalier, warming with his subject. "No one knew better than myself the immense struggle he laboured under; unless it was our good King, who supported him in all his arduous exertions. The Jesuists were his unrelenting antagonists; but they failed in their efforts to persuade the people that it was Pombal's edicts against their order which had brought this judgment upon the capital.

"Whilst the Court and the Royal Family dwelt in tents in the palace-gardens, and the earth continued to quake and tremble, almost it seemed, at the recollection of its own violence; whilst flames burst out at intervals, and the sea, which had risen between twenty and thirty feet, sank as low, leaving marshy pestiferous swamps, Pombal and his emissaries went about administering help, consolation, encouragement and advice. His wisdom and courage preserved the desolated city, which might, had all his great plans been carried out, have surpassed all other capitals in beauty, and have risen from its ashes the glory of the Peninsula.

"Along the banks of our noble river a string of palaces might have been erected, and the grandest promenade in Europe would have wound past verdant courts and gardens. Even as it was, the part of the city which had suffered most was speedily rebuilt, and made much more beautiful and healthy. Level, well-paved streets, wider and well-drained, replaced clumsy buildings and insalubrious lanes. Help poured in to us from all the cities of Europe, many of which had suffered, though less severely than ourselves."

"I have heard it said," observed Fraser, "that in our own mountain land a lake was formed by a simultaneous convulsion of nature. On that autumn day part of a great hill fell, damming up a river and changing its course. It still may be seen flowing through the centre of the loch, which expanded and filled the bed of the valley. Loch Lubnaig in Perthshire is said to date only from the time of your great earthquake in Lisbon. Can this be true?"

"No doubt, no doubt!" said the Doctor, who had listened attentively. "I have heard and read many strange tales about that All Saints' Day. I can only speak of what happened near me—that misery filled all my thoughts at the time. My wife, as you have seen, can scarcely bear to have it recalled to her memory. We had only been married three years, and were then, as we have ever since been, lovers. My only son was but two years old, Clara an infant safe, as we believed in her nursery.

"My wife and I, with most of the nobility, were in the Patriarchal Church in the square near the palace which then contained the Royal Chapel. The Court was in the country, providentially, for the wing of the palace usually occupied by the Royal Family was the first to fall. A great darkness suddenly hung over the high altar. I noticed some confusion among the clergy, who were in their purple robes; all was glitter and ornament, with bells ringing all over the city for the high festival.

"Madame always says she was not frightened till she saw me turn pale. I had been in our gold mines and diamond caves in Brazil, and knew the low rumble and oscillating movement which precedes an earth-quake, At once I hastened to draw her out of the crowd. In a moment it parted and scattered itself hither and thither. The priests left the rich jewels unguarded on the altar. No one touched them at first; but after the shock, some superstitious persons seized the relics, hoping, thereby, to win safety; but the veil or garment of a saintly woman, even the limb of a martyr, was of little avail and were soon cast away in despair.

"At last we got to the door. There I saw the river heave, and heard that the sea had risen, and that there was much damage among the shipping. A gulf opened and swallowed up the vessels; not a vestige of wreck was ever found. The new quay sank with thousands of people upon it. I got my wife away and we sped home to our darlings, whom we found safe in the garden with the nurses and slaves.

"Rozay has told you of Madame's heroism in searching out and standing by our blind aunt, while I was seeking all over the palace in despair for other members of the family. I did not know of her peril till it was past; but, long afterwards, the market-women used to kiss her garments as she went by. That shock was the very last severe one, though the earth vibrated for many a day. I have been in many lands subject to these visitations, but I have never seen anything like it. If Lisbon had been so near to the sea as Lima it would have been overwhelmed; as that great city was in 1746, when its waves rose and destroyed the lower part of the town."

The Chevalier paused, overcome with emotion, presently he went on:

"After that dread time we were at peace, and recovered gradually from our alarm; repaired, with the liberal aid of the government, our wrecked palaces and houses, and dwelt under our lemon and orange groves, and fig-trees. My family were sharers in a great palace partly occupied by a nobleman; who, after being at one time in high favour at Court, fell into only well-deserved disgrace, and suffered the barbarous punishment due to high treason. Even his wife's grey hairs were not respected, their sons perished miserably, their daughters and daughters-in-law were immured in convents. Perhaps the guilty cause of all their woe—the faithless wife and heartless woman who was said to have won the King's favour—had the easiest lot; though she too was shut up in a nunnery of a less strict order, and banished for ever from Court.

"I shall not dwell on that side of the question, but only tell what may be necessary to account for my banishment. There was an agreement between the two families to light up the great hall which we used in common, alternately. Whether by accident or malice prepense, on one night when it should have been kept dark to further a sovereign's pleasure, the lamps were lit; and betrayed his passage to the private carriage which was waiting for him.

Shortly afterwards a foul plan was laid to murder him, which was baffled by his own promptitude in ordering the coachman to turn back, after he had passed the first relay of assassins.

"Had he gone on, six bullets might have pierced his royal person. As it was, he was severely wounded. The conspirators were all seized, their plots baffled, and a cruel vengeance overtook the whole brood.

"Pombal, still my friend, but the stern avenger of his Sovereign's attempted murder, warned me that my near neighbourhood to the chief conspirator, and some efforts I had made in behalf of a member of a family whom I had believed to be innocent, had exposed me to suspicion. I had but a few hours in which to prepare for flight; and, as you have heard, the child Rozay was taken off to sea with us. We fled to England; later on I brought my family to America.

"My wife's tender heart yearns still for her native land, but I am happy here; and, as I share my great Master's horror of superstition, I prefer these fertile meads on the banks of Savannah, to the priest-ridden capitals of Southern Europe."

Clara's colour had returned to her cheeks, and her eyes were bright with happiness, when they gathered round the simple repast spread in the saloon. She no longer glanced with a shudder at the rapidly-flowing river, which now reflected a brilliant sunset. Though many years have passed since that blooming girl hid her lover's letter in her bosom—that letter which told her he should soon be with her to claim her plighted troth, is still extant. Its faded lines still tell the same tale of warm love and ardent loyalty as when her heart beat against it that evening. Some trifle had delayed his journey—but, no matter, he was safe and had escaped the hurricane. The young life was preserved, to which her own was irrevocably bound; before long, she trusted, he would be with her.

"Tell dear Rozay," may still be read by her grandchildren in that simple touching letter, "that our happiness would not be complete without her. I am making a home for you both. Some day the Chevalier and Madame will return to Portugal where they have many ties and friends; her heart still owns no other allegiance. And then, if Rozay does not marry, which you will say is most unlikely, she must settle with us at our farm, near Augusta city, in the fertile meads where flowers are blooming and crops waving; and we will show the old benighted world where the sun shines so coldly, how warm and true, in this southern clime love can be!"

In such, or nearly such words, full of bright hopes and dreams, the young planter wooed his bride, and strove to reconcile to the change which was fast approaching in her destiny, the young sister-like cousin whose maiden meditations he believed to be as yet entirely fancy free.

CHAPTER X.

Well knows the fair and friendly moon
    The band that Marion leads,
The glitter of their rifles,
    The trampling of their steeds!
'Tis life our fiery barbs to guide
    Across the moonlit plains;
'Tis life to feel the night wind
    That lifts their tossing manes;
A moment in the ravaged camp,
    A moment, and away,
Back to the pathless forest
    Before the peep of day!

The Chevalier and his dark-eyed daughter, with her fair inseparable companion, Rozay Morais, rode down the next morning with their guests to the ford over the river; and after seeing them across, and accompanying them for some distance, returned to Casa Bianca.

The young men had received ample instructions respecting their route, and they were also furnished with a pass written in, and adorned with, certain cabalistic characters and signs which would be recognised and honoured by the Indians, and would probably, if left in their hands, be regarded as a prescription and treasured as a charm in cases of sickness.

The country was reported as quiet, but it was quite on the cards that Marion's band instead of being at Ox-swamp - where he had by a daring assault defeated a large body of royalist troops who were caught in a trap in a narrow causeway blocked by felled trees—might now be fifty miles from that place. The night-marches undertaken in the face of all obstacles, and often quite unintelligible even to those who executed them blindly, generally led to success as unaccountable as it was unexpected.

These warriors of the swamp and jungle with their victorious leader seemed proof against all arms, discipline, and numbers. Often a mere handful of men would sweep down some hitherto unknown forest glade, many miles from the place where they had been last seen or heard of, and dashing into the enemy's camp among the sleeping bewildered soldiery, would deal death and destruction before they made their way back, like wild animals to their impenetrable lair.

The moon was shining down from a cloudless sky when our little troop of horsemen approached the spot where they had been advised to halt for the night; a lone house on the outskirts of a forest. One of the many tributaries of the larger river they had crossed in the morning flowed through the plain. The low light was reflected in the water and caught the white walls of the deserted building, which might, they had been told, though empty and solitary, afford temporary shelter.

But, on this occasion, it did not look quite deserted.

Light shone out from a small window, and a horse neighed in the compound. Other travellers appeared to have been beforehand with them, and those were not days in which it was safe to make chance acquaintance with wayfarers. On the other hand, these might be peaceful strangers and afford pleasant companionship, or even help in case of danger.

The sudden challenge of an outpost and the click of a gunlock dispelled the feeling of tranquility inspired by the moonlit repose of the landscape. The light in the window was obscured, and out of the earth as it seemed rose dusky figures barring the road. The officers were surrounded, but without incivility. All that was required was that they should surrender themselves into the hands of their captors and accompany them to their leader's quarters.

Resistance was out of the question, since every bush seemed to have concealed an armed man. More than fifty lean but stalwart fellows—dressed in leather jerkins and with felt caps pulled low on their swarthy brows, looking more like hunters than warriors—closed round the travellers. The best, the only plan, seemed to be to follow them quietly and make terms with their chief.

A long series of successful fights in the jungles and marshy forests of Savannah had raised the Guerilla chief's fame to its highest pitch. Captain Conyers, one of his famous brigade, in a hand-to-hand fight, had slain a British colonel. At Black-Mungo Swamp the band had stood with reversed arms by the open grave of their less fortunate but

equally brave comrade, Charlie Logan, and sworn to re-
venge his fall after riding eighty miles to rejoin them. Here
the general had captured his glorious chestnut steed, now
stabled in the compound at the back of what had once
been a farmhouse but was now little more than a ruin.

Marion's grave face, full of stern resolution, and of grief
for the friend and comrade whose loss he most severely
felt, was bent over some papers, which he was intently
studying by the light of the candle which the travellers
had seen burning in the window, when they were ushered
into his presence. Though they were wrapped in common
riding-cloaks, which quite hid their uniforms, his quick
eye perceived at a glance that they were British officers;
and, at that moment, their position did not stand them
in good stead. Charlie Logan had fallen under the thrust
of a British bayonet—his life-blood had dyed the soil trodden by the invader. Marion set his teeth hard, and
groaned inwardly as he detected the proud Islanders in
their rough travelling-garb, and classed them with the
murderers of his comrade, the enslavers of his country.

"Your name and rank in the service?" he said curtly.
"Your best course is to be perfectly candid. I know that
you belong to the Royal army. When did you leave the
camp? What was your object?"

"To break fresh ground, as sportsmen call it," replied
Fraser, in an open manly way. "We do not deny that we
are officers belonging to the Royal army. Our name and
rank are put down in this pass by our friend Doctor Lu-

cena of Casa Bianca, where we have been staying. It was given us to be shown to any Indian we might meet. Our purpose, as you may guess by the size of our party, was not hostile."

Marion took the scroll. A grim smile passed over his dark face as he perused it, and scanned the allegorical signs with which it was embellished.

"The Chevalier Lucena is a good man," he said as he returned it; "one of God's saints, and the ladies of his family are angels. This was meant to protect you from savages; perhaps the hard treatment we have met with may have made us little better. Good and bad, white skin or red, loyalist or rebel, as you call us, if they are sick or sorrowful, wounded or destitute, find refuge and healing at Casa Bianca."

Marion paused for a moment, and added in a grave, at the same time more friendly tone:

"He is, moreover, of no party, no man's enemy, everybody's friend. Gentlemen, if circumstances have made us savages, we have the virtues of those unfortunate outcasts—hospitality—fidelity to the hand that has healed us. You shall have food and shelter. After that, when the night ends, I will give you a guide for some distance. These swamps are dangerous. Now, farewell, till the evening meal, to which I invite you, is ready."

The Guerilla leader made a slight but courteous gesture of leave-taking, and was absorbed in his occupation before the officers quitted the room. As he bent his dark face over the papers, the light on the table flashed upon the silver crescent in front of his cap, as we have said, once the gorget of a British officer, bringing out the word "Liberty" engraved upon it; leaving the remainder of the inscription "or Death" in deep shadow.

This was the man who helped greatly in winning the independence of the Colonies, and on whose tomb at Belle Isle, near the "broad Santee," is recorded by his grateful country-men that he lived and died without fear and without reproach.

The woodman's craft was shown in the abundant though simple repast served up an hour later. The venison steaks were admirably cooked with sauce made from berries which abounded in the district and the birds wrapped in leaves and baked in clay among the wood ashes seemed to the tired wanderers much more delicious than any dish ever tasted at their mess-table.

Marion ate little and scarcely spoke, but the few words he uttered during the repast were gracious and to the purpose. His parting sentences remained engraven on the memory of his guests long after they were, probably, by himself forgotten.

"No doubt," he said, as they rose from the table, "you were not sent into the haunts of the Swamp-Fox for nothing—but there is little to discover! We are men without homes, without stores, without visible resources. Here to-day, gone to-morrow - the birds of the air, the fish in the river, leave as little mark of their passage! We have few ties, we are wanderers on the face of God's earth like our great Master—often with no place to lay down our weary heads, nor a hole to creep into and hide in."

He looked up quickly with a bright flash in his eyes at the young officers, as he went on speaking.

"But we do not disband, as I have read and heard that your Highland clans do after battle, and carry home the spoils. As I said, we have no homes and want no riches. We have, instead, a great purpose which we shall live to see fulfilled. We want Freedom—equal rights—just laws—exemption from taxes and military oppression. When men like ourselves have cast to the winds life, ease, comfort, domestic happiness, and want only justice—depend upon it, sooner or later, they will have their desire—or, dying, they will leave its fruition to their children"

He left the room after a quiet but courteous salutation, returning to his solitary occupation.

The light in the window burnt on till long after midnight, while, carefully sentinelled, the woodland camp was at rest. Mackenzie woke at the still hour of the dawn and fancied that he heard the rapid tramp of horse-hoofs borne away by the wind. It was bitterly cold, and, pulling his cloak around him, he soon dropped off to sleep again.

When morning was fully come, he got up and looked from the window. Had he dreamed that he sat at supper with the famous Guerilla leader whose exploits were the topic of the day, and that he lay down to sleep in the midst of his leaguer?

There was not a sign of the recent presence of a troop of horsemen under the waving boughs of the forest, which came down nearly to the water's edge. Not a sod of turf had been turned nor a branch broken. The ruinous farm-house and buildings might have been entirely deserted since the day when the Indians broke in upon the slumber of its inmates, and ravaged their peaceful home, as Mackenzie had been told at the supper-table.

But in the crazy outhouse, which had served the purpose of a stable, the horses were safe, and had been plentifully supplied with food; enough remaining to furnish a morning meal before starting, as well as for the mid-day halt. The attendants had also been well cared for and Fraser and Mackenzie found ample provision for their own wants laid out on the table where Marion had bent over the despatches which, probably, told him where to find a slumbering foe on the next night. He and his band were gone, and as far as possible all signs of their presence obliterated. They had swept off through the forest in the early dawn, and were now far away on their course.

After the officers had breakfasted, they mounted their horses, and rode for some distance along the banks of the river. Marion had not forgotten any of his promises; at a short distance from the ruined farm-house they found a silent but trusty guide, who led them through the intricacies of the marshy forest-land which, otherwise, would have been difficult to traverse. Their mid-day meal was taken in the shade of the greenwood, where the forester left them, saying that if they pursued the track he had put them upon till it struck a wider and more defined path, it would lead them before nightfall to the British camp.

Meanwhile, at Casa Bianca, the day had passed somewhat heavily away; and, in the evening especially, their military guests were missed by all inmates. The Chevalier and Madame played at some quiet game and retired early to bed, but the two girls sat up long in the veranda, watching the moon as she travelled slowly across the unclouded heavens.

The river went past them with a song; and some nightbirds warbled among the low bushes and reeds, which emitted a murmuring whisper as the wind passed through their tall spear-shaped heads. The frogs joined in the concert, but the girls were silent and some-what sad.

Rozay seemed to have lost her high spirits, and complained of fatigue; though a much longer ride than they had taken in pleasant company that morning did not usually tire her. The fact was, as her, on the present occasion, more lively companion perceived, she was grave and dull in consequence of their visitors' departure. In their quiet life on Savannah's bank there were not often such agreeable breaks in the monotony of their domestic pursuits.

To divert her cousin's thoughts Clara read to her parts of her lover's last letter, but somehow, it seemed as if Rozay entered less cordially than usual into the idea of sharing their home and anticipated happiness.

She felt sure she should be terribly in the way, and

would not hear of making a third in the young Planter's dwelling. If she was doomed to be an old maid, as was most likely in these fearful times, when the young men ran terrible risks of being killed in battle; and if indeed her adopted parents did not want her more than ever when their own child left them, as she believed would be the case, she would live alone in a hut in the woods, with her cat and her parrot.

Clara put back her letter into its usual resting-place, and gave up that attempt at conversation. She was more successful when she talked about the two officers who had just left them, and made Rozay tell her all about that she and George Mackenzie had talked about, while she and Major Fraser rode on with her father through the woods after crossing the ford.

Launched on this subject, Rozay spoke more freely, and after a time merrily enough. Clara was surprised to find how much she knew of their late companion's history. George was unaccustomed to sympathy, and when he saw the girl's eyes full of tears at the tale of his home trials, to which he had accidentally alluded, and emptied his soul of his troubles. Rozay knew all about Morag and Donald and the old Scottish Castle by Beauly Water—the nights spent in the woods, and the enlistment, after the fire at the little Inn in the village.

Major Fraser had not been half so communicative, probably not having received the same encouragement, but he had talked a good deal about his friend. Rozay listened attentively to what Clara told her of his popularity in the regiment, his distinguished gallantry and military talent. His promotion had been rapid and he had performed important services for which his discretion had procured his appointment. After beginning his career in the ranks, he was likely to rise to high places. The men of the regiment, too, regarded him as a friend, his ears were always open to any just complaint: while at the same time, no officer was more exact as to maintaining discipline and in requiring prompt obedience to orders.

The topic being at last exhausted the two girls retired for the night, but more than once, while her cousin was sleeping (they always from childhood had shared the same room), Rozay, still feverish and restless, stole from her couch and went to the open window, to look out at the tranquil scene in the quiet cool night.

The moon, high in the heavens, which as usual, except in case of sudden tempests, were quite unclouded, shone down into the calm broad river. The leaves scarcely rustled, only the bull-frogs croaked and the insects hummed and buzzed, in that warm, scented atmosphere.

Little did she suspect, as Rozay Morais leant from the window, and surveyed that still prospect, that beyond the wood and river among the well-nigh impenetrable swamps and dense forests, the man whom she did not yet acknowledge to be her lover, though she had from the first been drawn to him, was lying down to sleep in the midst of Marion's lawless band—the Guerillas and their dauntless leader.

As it was she uttered, under her breath, a fervent prayer for his safety, and though only the night wind caught the sound, she blushed as deeply as though the breeze would waft it to her lover. She had almost owned him to be one by this time, and she did not envy her adopted sister, as she had for a few brief moments felt inclined to do when listening to portions of Philip Lavigne's warm-hearted letter.

And so at length Rozay too lay down to rest, and slept soundly till the morning by her cousin's side, each alike unconscious and unmindful of any trial which might be in store for them in the future, while the bright clear river flowed on past forest, swamp, and city, to its vent in ocean, regardless of the wreck and consternation caused but yesterday, when it broke its banks and deluged the land, breaking all barriers in its sudden fury.

Oh! fair and glorious rivers lying in light, golden and crimson in the sunset, silvery under moonbeams, do ye ever grieve over the wreaths carried away by your cruel water—cast out to perish unheeded on some shining river or left, like Ella's roses, to wither upon the oozy bank.

PART THE THIRD.

"Nay, grieve not for the dead alone,
    Whose song has told their heart's sad story,-
Weep for the voiceless, who have known
    The cross without the crown of glory,
Not where Leucadian breezes sweep
    O'er Sappho's memory-haunted billow,
But where the glittering night-dews weep
    On nameless sorrow's churchyard pillow.

"Oh hearts that break and give no sign
    Save whitening lip, and fading tresses,
Till Death pours out his cordial wine
    Slow-dropped from Misery's crushing presses.
If singing breath or echoing chord
    To every hidden pang were given,
What endless melodies were poured,
    As sad as earth, as sweet as heaven!"

OLIVER WENDELL HOLMES.

CHAPTER XI.

Dead sienna and rusty gold,
  Tell the year in the marsh is old:
Black and bent the sedges shrink
  Back from the sea-pool's frosty brink.
Low in the west a wind-cloud lies,
  Tossed and wild in the autumn skies.
Over the marshes, mournfully,
  Drifts the sound of the restless sea.

Many months had passed away in desultory warfare among the swamps through which flow the Pedee and Santee, before Mackenzie and Fraser were at liberty to revisit Casa Bianca; but they had not forgotten, and they were well remembered by, its inmates. At last, with some difficulty, the two officers obtained leave to attend the marriage festivities of the Chevalier's daughter and the young planter, Philip Lavigne.

The broad river was heavily swollen, and the sky thick with rain, when the two Highlanders crossed the ford. An hour or two later, and some persons who were anxiously watching the rising flood, said that it would not be safe to pass over it; a bridge many miles up the stream would have to be resorted to by the expected bridegroom and his friend.

The white house was lit up, and the veranda garlanded by the hands of the young girls with autumn leaves and berries. The gorgeous tints of the American foliage seemed almost to illuminate the wide, cool place of shelter, where the guests were more frequently received than in the saloon. Rozay and Clara, dressed alike and in white, were fastening a few clusters of choice flowers—the last of the decorations—in appropriate positions, when their guests from the camp arrived. They each spared a flower, and gave it with a bright blush to greet them. Rozay's white blossom fell to the share of George Mackenzie, who playfully received it, like a knight of old, on bended knee. The bride gave hers to Fraser.

A cloud rested on her brow the next moment, when allusion was made to the rapid rise of the river, and the probable delay in the arrival of their expected visitors.

"Oh, I hope Philip will be patient, and not attempt to cross the ford!" she said, trembling as though a cold blast reached her, whilst she drew back the heavy curtain and looked out on the troubled grey sky. "He ought to have been here an hour ago."

Rozay tried to reassure her. Most likely other streams had risen, interposing obstacles in his way. He was sure to come soon—before the night fell.

It grew darker even as she spoke, and a wilder gust swept through the veranda, shaking some of the petals from the flowers. Clara dropped the curtain with a sigh.

The ceremony was to take place at mid-night; and all who were expected to take part in it, or act as spectators only, were already assembled, when Mackenzie and Fraser entered the large saloon—all except the most important persons, the bridegroom and his friend. The priest was talking in a low voice, encouragingly to Clara, who looked in her white robes like a beautiful statue. She sat quite still, near the entrance; but not withstanding her apparently fixed attention, there was a listening air, as if she were hearing something beyond—much farther off than the holy father's words.

Suddenly she started forward, dropping the nosegay of white scented-flowers Rozay had made up for her.

"They are coming," she said. "But, oh what a noise the river makes - drowning the sound of their foot-steps!"

No one else had distinguished any sound from outside, except the low, melancholy murmur of the wind, and rain falling heavily but monotonously, as it had done since the night set in.

Several gentlemen rose and left the room. A sudden gloom fell on the company. There was no token of any fresh arrival.

Clara remained standing, as if arrested by some inward sensation, on the same spot. She pushed back her dark hair, and looked anxiously round.

"Did no one else hear him? It was Philip—I could not be mistaken. He called me twice!"

The Priest and the Chevalier endeavoured to soothe

her, assuring her that her affianced lover would soon join her, but that she could not have heard his voice. All the windows were closed, and no one had approached the house.

"I shall never hear his voice again!" she said sadly. "But we shall soon be together. Philip has called me from the other world!"

Her tall, slight form swayed; and, but for her father's arm cast tenderly around her, she would have fallen—but she did not faint. Rozay stood by her whispering consolation; but her words were unheard. Every sense was strained; waiting for the sound of a voice, the touch of a hand, which yet she well knew she would never, in life, hear or feel again.

Mackenzie and Fraser and other young men of the party were, meanwhile, on their way to the ford. Blackly the night closed round them; the dull roar of the flooded river grew louder; the only lights seen, seemed to come no one knew whence, catching the whirling flakes of foaming water.

Alas, the lover's impatience had spurned the counsels of the more experienced friend who accompanied him, and the loiterers on the banks of the stream. He had ridden his horse down to the ford, believing it to be still practicable, while his more prudent companion, declining to follow his rash example, had gone on to the bridge. Horse and man had been swept away by the boiling flood. The voice which Clara alone had heard—if indeed it uttered her loved name—had spoken it in the last moment, ere the rushing river silenced its tones for ever.

A very mournful party gathered in the white house on that stormy November evening. All they could do, and that was attended with great risk, was to bring the lifeless form of the bridegroom to the home of the bride.

Clara shed no tears, and spoke no wild words of grief. Despair is dumb; and her heart found no relief in outward demonstrations. The wound bled inwardly. But she was still unselfish. Her father and mother clung to her, and were not unheeded. Rozay wept till she could weep no more. Clara silently caressed and comforted them. If she made her moan—if she wept, it was when, at her own earnest request, she was left in the still hours of the early morning to watch alone by her dead lover—on whose breast she had placed Rozay's bunch of late-blowing, sweet-scented white roses.

At the earnest request of the Chevalier and Madame Lucena, the two young officers who had rescued Philip Lavigne's helpless, lifeless form from the whirling flood which would otherwise have borne it down to the sea, remained to attend the funeral, with some of the other guests.

Clara would not leave him. As she might have stood by his side at the altar, clad in white bridal robes, she now walked beside his coffin to his last earthly resting-place. Rozay and her girl friends, also dressed in white, accompanied her. In the simple burial-ground belonging to the station, Philip Lavigne, with his young bride bending over him, was lowered to the grave. Some flowers were thrown in, many tears fell, and then the mourning friends went back to the white house; and sadly took down the till then forgotten faded garlands which the girls had hung up with light hearts, in readiness for Clara's bridal.

There are some hearts that are drawn closer by affliction shared faithfully together, and such were those of the sister-cousins. Never in after life was that communion relaxed. In joy and sorrow they were united. Though many changes awaited them, though other ties and other homes received them, all were shared together. To the day of their deaths Rozay Morais and Clara Lucena were like sisters; nor did they ever, amid their changing fortunes, forget the stormy night when the wild winds of Autumn and the roaring flood of the American River, sweeping away leaf and blossom, young life and budding hope, converted the gay preparations for Clara and Philip's espousals into the sad precursors of his untimely fate.

CHAPTER XII.

I was not half worthy of you, Douglas,
  Not half worthy the like of you;-
Now all men beside are to me but shadows,
  Douglas, Douglas, tender and true.

While Clara, in her silent grief, kept herself se-cluded, and the few friends who lingered till the solemn rites were over, one after another quietly departed, Rozay Morais, for the first time excluded, wandered sor-rowfully and alone by the brimming river. Now that it had wrought its work of mischief, it flowed on calmly, reflect-ing unclouded sunshine.

Mackenzie had bid adieu to his host and hostess; but while his friend completed some slight preparations for departure, he went out, desiring the soldier servant, who had charge of their horses and portmanteaus, to lead his charger to the ferry where he would meet them; the river having subsided as quickly as it had risen, sufficiently to make the shorter passage safe.

The young Highlander's quick eye had caught sight of a girl's figure in the wood which went down to the water-side, and in the soft mould was the print of a small slender foot (matching a tiny slipper still in our possession) which he would have recognised anywhere.

Rozay had cast herself down on a felled trunk overhung with trailing wild vine; and was gazing through tears at the river which had borne away in its wild overflow the hopes of two lives.

"How quietly it glides along, now," she said, greeting Mackenzie with a sad smile as he stood beside her. "Oh, who would think our own bright shining water could have been so cruel! I am afraid Clara will never care to look on it again."

"Do you think that your sweet sister-cousin will retain any implacable feeling?" said Mackenzie, gently, as he ventured to place himself beside her on the tree trunk, Rozay having moved a little to make room for him. "Nature is our best consoler, impassive as she is. Perhaps that is one reason why her calmness soothes us even in our wildest grief. My saddest hours were spent by Beauly Water, which often mocked me by its sunshiny serenity; but I love the remembrance of my native hills, and glens, and lochs, and I would wish to stand beside our Firth were dark clouds to weigh as heavily on my heart as they often have done on its shores."

Rozay listened with interest, as she always did when the Highlander with kindling glance spoke of his native land.

"You love Scotland, and yet I have heard that the climate is cold and the soil in many parts sterile; you have, too, known little but sorrow in your early home. I am an orphan and cannot remember father or mother, or my birthplace. Clara's parents have been mine; she is like a sister; and these luxuriant landscapes are very dear, but they are not like home."

She paused, sighing. Mackenzie took the little hand which clasped the vine-tendrils.

"Neither have I a home, or near kindred except my poor old father, and my adopted brother and sister," he said, tenderly. "But Rozay, we have the world before us. When I have made myself a name, when, in some corner of my bonnie native land—it is not all cold and barren— there is some spot that calls me master, be it cottage or castle, will you share it with me?"

The girl turned her blushing face away, but she did not withdraw her hand.

"Oh, I cannot talk of happiness today—not when Clara is in such sorrow," she said, her voice breaking.

"Then it would be happiness, Rozay?" said Mackenzie, striving to look into her averted face. "I shall not forget that admission. At this moment I dare not, I will not press you to give me an answer. But do not forget me!"

He rose as he spoke. Rozay trembled so much that she could not, when she tried at his earnest entreaty to walk with him through the wood towards the ford, move without assistance. Mackenzie drew her hand through his arm.

"Let me support you, dear one, now and ever," he said. "When I next visit Casa Bianca it will be to ask your guardian's permission to woo you for my bride. I dare not intrude my hopes upon him now."

They walked slowly between the tall trees, till they came to the end of the wood. At but a short distance was the ferry where his friend and the horses were waiting for him.

Rozay drew back when the path terminated, and with one fond betrothal kiss, Mackenzie left her to return alone to Casa Bianca.

The young officer met with no adventures this time while returning to camp. They knew the road, and Marion and his band were far away.

It might partly be owing to the new hope which had sprung up in the midst of sorrow that Mackenzie's thoughts fixed themselves more strongly than had lately been the case on his future prospects. Ever since Fraser brought him Morag's letter imploring him to return home, he had felt that he ought, if possible, to be on the spot to counteract the machinations of his enemies: but his military duties imperatively chained him to the regiment, while engaged in arduous active service.

There came, however, a lull in the war, and he asked and obtained leave to return to Scotland on urgent private business - the more easily as a neglected injury caused by the wind of a spent ball scathing his chest, received in the last battle which was likely to take place during this campaign, occasioned him much pain and inconvenience. Fraser was also allowed an interval of leisure; and the two friends, at the commencement of the cold season when the army went into winter quarters, returned together on leave to their native land.

After a week spent pleasantly among the Frasers, who were all glad to hear tidings of their kinsmen in the Highland regiments raised not long before service in the Colonies, the two inseparable companions found themselves staying at the little Inn near the Beauly Water where Mackenzie had taken the King's shilling from the Sergeant.

Rumours of a very unpleasant nature respecting proceedings at Redcastle had reached him, but he refused to believe them. He was determined to see with his own eyes and hear with his own ears, before he stigmatised his father's wife as one unworthy of the name, and asserted his claim as "Muckle Colin's" heir to prevent the utter ruin of the property.

The Beauly Water rippled close to his feet; the woods, now leafless and covered with sparkling rime, glittered in the pale winter sunshine, when Mackenzie once more saw through the trees the red-sandstone walls of his early home. He had despatched a trusty messenger to invite Morag and Donald to meet him at what Fraser persisted in calling "Morag's fairy glen," though it bore in the locality a quite different name.

It wanted some hours yet of the appointed time when they had agreed to go together to the rendezvous. George was pacing up and down, alone and impatiently, the opposite strand. He was not thinking of the past, but of the future. That future which he hoped Rozay Morais would share with him.

The American song-birds were flitting through the trailing parasites by the flooded river, the gurgle of the water among the bulrushes sounded in his ear louder than the soft note of the English robin; yet nearer still in his heart of hearts, was the image of a girl, a foreigner, an orphan; and her sweet low voice was whispering to him as he walked by the Beauly Water, that she, like himself, was sad and lonely.

And yet, yonder, above the wood, was a fair castle which one day by right might be his own—a bonnie nest for his Lusitanian nightingale, if the elements of war and the schemes of wicked men and artful women gave up to the Scottish youth, when his time came, the good lands to which he was the undoubted heir.

Fraser's voice, reminding him of the hour, dispelled his reverie, and they set off together to walk round by the winding shore to the spot where a boat waited in readiness to bear them across the Beauly Firth.

CHAPTER XIII.

"When Eve had led her lord away,
  And Cain had killed his brother,
The stars and flowers, the poets say,
  Agreed with one another

"To cheat the cunning tempter's art,
  And teach the race its duty,
By keeping on his wicked heart
  Their eyes of love and beauty.

"A million sleepless lids, they say,
  Will be at least a warning;-
And so the flowers would watch by day,
  The stars from eve till morning."

OLIVER WENDELL HOLMES.

Those sleepless eyes of night were twinkling in the frosty haze which hung above the water, and the trees stood motionless with their leafless branches stretched across the pathway, when Morag came swiftly along it to meet her adopted brother. Donald was pursuing his studies at the University in Edinburgh.

"He says he means to be a lawyer and take care of your interests, George," the girl said; when after a tender embrace, Mackenzie enquired after her usually constant companion, while Morag was timidly returning Fraser's greeting. "His military ardour cooled after you left us; and he thinks now, that one soldier is enough for the country to have from our home. He has a long head people say, and an eloquent tongue, and will make a capital pleader."

"Well," said George, laughing, "he was an obstinate young fellow, and loved a tough argument almost as well as a tussle with a big fish. That was more to his taste than law when I left home. But Morag, what of my father?"

The girl's voice was very sad and low, as she answered him.

"Oh George, I am afraid he is wearing away—mind and body. He looks like the shadow of what even I can remember him. But I see him very rarely. My mother is devoted to him; and he cares for nothing now but to have her with him."

"She deals kindly with him, I trust?" said young Mackenzie anxiously;-rumour having informed him that "Muckle Colin" was shut up by his braw wife;" and that no one knew what passed within the of late secluded precincts of Redcastle.

"Oh there is no doubt about my mother treating your poor father kindly;" said Morag, with some surprise. "He worships the ground she treads upon, and cannot bear her to be, even for half an hour, away from him. We see no company now, except some of our own kindred," she added, gravely. "Your father is not able for it. His mind has failed very much since you left home."

"Does he miss me?" said George with deep feeling. "If I thought so, Morag, I would abjure my oath not to enter my father's house until summoned there by its master."

"I cannot tell—he never names you," said Morag, slowly; her voice breaking as if tears choked it.

"But there were signs of love," said George. "You told me, and I have never forgotten it, that when I went away he looked at my empty place at the table, and patted my dog's head. You thought he sorrowed for my absence, at first. Has he forgotten me?"

"He forgets everything," said Morag mournfully. "When Donald went away he seemed sorry for a moment; but it passed. He has never once asked for him, or cared to see his letters, or hear them read. I know that my mother proposed it, and was vexed by his indifference!"

"She would not remind him of my claim to his affection;" said George, bitterly. "And yet I am his only son and heir! Morag it is a hard thing to come home and find no welcome waiting for me!"

"I do think that my mother has changed," said Morag, hesitatingly. "When she heard that you were staying with Major Fraser's family, she asked me if you were coming here, - to Redcastle, I mean. Will you not forget your foolish vow, George, and return home?"

"It does not seem like home to me, now," said the young officer, sadly. "But I will write, I will make some arrangement for a meeting with your mother, or—what I desire far more—for seeing my father. Now I am afraid I must leave you. My wound pains me strangely. I am not the boy I was. The cold of these northern frosty nights searches me cruelly."

"How you tremble, George," said Morag, pressing the arm she held. "I did not know you had been wounded?"

She turned to Fraser, as though she felt that George needed assistance, stronger than she could give him, and herself fuller information.

"Yes; he has been ill," said his friend. "Though it was the wind only of a spent ball which grazed his chest, the Doctor says he may feel it all his life, - the scar will never be effaced. He has suffered much and needs rest and soothing. All emotion is bad for him."

Fraser had come closer to them while he spoke, and his friend willingly accepted his support. Morag walked with them to the loch shore where the boat waited; and then returned with an anxious heart, through the wintry woods by a nearer way to the Castle.

A sever attack of fever prevented Mackenzie's overtures for reconciliation. He was confined to his bed many days, at times delirious, at others restless and exhausted. As soon as his friend could make up his mind to leave him he went up to the mansion, where his reception was much more gracious than he expected.

Mrs. Mackenzie regretted deeply that the state of her husband's mental and bodily health prevented his receiving any visitors. Excitement had the worst possible effect on him. Even his son, she feared, could not at the present time be permitted to see him, even if he were well enough to make the change of quarters which she hoped he contemplated. It was painful to think that the heir of the house should be lying ill at a village Inn so near his home.

Her manner and whole appearance were quiet and subdued. Fraser thought her changed since he had seen her surrounded by company. Perhaps what propitiated him most was that she no longer discouraged his attentions to her fair young daughter. Her mind seemed entirely engrossed with the care of her invalid husband, whose state, she said, became daily more distressing. He required incessant watchfulness.

As he rode away, Fraser saw the melancholy old giant at a distance throwing stones, like a boy, into the water. His great strength was gone. The arm which had tossed the caber, and launched the curling-stone on its icy path, could now scarcely lift the pebbles which he threw but a short way to amuse the dog that followed him. All the comfort he could carry back to his friend was that the faithful colley who accompanied his father was, Morag told him, George's old favourite.

The little Inn by the waterside was now managed by old servants who formerly lived at the Castle—the butler, who had thrown up his situation when he heard his young master insulted at the dining-table, and George's nurse. He was tenderly served, and every possible comfort provided for him which circumstances permitted. Mrs. Mackenzie herself sent delicacies to tempt his languid appetite, with flowers from the conservatories; but George cared little for them.

Only the flowers Morag gathered, the grapes her hands had touched, were acceptable. Some instinct, or rather some ineradicable prejudice, prevented his placing trust in his fair but false enemy. There are so many good second mothers in families that it is grievous to have to dwell on an exceptional case. Many women, in our own limited experience, take to their hearts with motherly love the desolate children who have lost their own parents. All honour be to them! Praise and love wait on their path! blessings be about their homes and hearths!

Such there are, such there have been, and such there will be, while women with warm hearts and honest minds live in our midst, and take compassion on those who are left alone, forlorn and helpless; but such a woman's heart did not beat in the breast of the lady of Redcastle—Muckle Colin's second wife.

Major Fraser, having neither instinct nor prejudice to guide or mislead him, took her to be what it was her pleasure to seem—a pleasant, comely matron. He did not refuse the frequent invitations to Redcastle; since, besides enabling him to convey information to his friend, these visits afforded him opportunities for ingratiating himself not only with Morag, but with her mother.

Once or twice he was permitted a glimpse of the old Laird, who seemed sullen and dull. He never adverted to his own or his wife's son, or seemed to recollect Fraser;

though Mrs. Mackenzie declared she had told him he was a brother-in-arms of George, who had returned with him to Scotland. When George's illness was alluded to he did not speak. Apparently his heir might die at the Highland Inn without stirring the sluggish pulses of the old Laird.

Many tokens of kindness from other quarters, far and near, were showered on the invalid officer. From his devoted nurse to the highest landed gentry in the district, his friends and neighbours, rich and poor, were delighted to have him once more among them.

Mackenzie, however, when he became at last convalescent, accepted no invitations. Until he could enter as a welcome guest, invited by his father, the home of his ancestors, he cared to visit no other house; and Muckle Colin gave no sign of affection. At the end of some weeks, weary of vain expectation, Mackenzie went to the gates of Redcastle and asked permission to see his father; but a short stern message precluding his entrance, was sent, purporting to come from the head of the house. His son had gone away and disgraced himself by enlisting as a common soldier in the ranks, and he might stay away as long as he liked. There was no place for him there.

While Mackenzie hesitated, Morag came out, breathless with agitation. Her mother had sent her to say that the Laird was beside himself with anger. She dared not leave him. On the mention of his son's name and wish to see him, such a tempest of rage had swept over the old giant that it momentarily restored his strength. The servants had fled in terror. Such another attack, his wife feared, even her soothing powers might not allay. She implored her stepson to have patience. When a gentler humour came upon his father, she would not fail to summon him to Redcastle.

CHAPTER XIV.

"O'er hill and prairie, field and lawn,
    Their dewy eyes upturning,
The flowers still watch from reddening dawn
    Till western skies are burning.

"Alas! each hour of daylight tells
    A tale of shame so crushing
That some turn white as sea-bleached shells,
    And some are always blushing.

"But when the patient stars look down
    O'er all, their light discovers,
The traitor's smile, the murderer's frown,
    The lips of lying lovers.

"They try to shut their saddening eyes,
    And in the vain endeavour,
We see them twinkling in the skies,
    And so they blink for ever."

               OLIVER WENDELL HOLMES.

If George had seen his old father walking feebly by the loch side with the faithful colley at his heels, neither of them seeming to have spirit enough to throw a stone or stick into, or bring it back out of the water, he would scarcely have given credence to the report of his fiery burst of rage half an hour before.

The young heir might also have seen, in the embrasure of a window overlooking the domain which was surely but slowly passing away from him, a couple of figures, busy with parchments and title deeds which deeply concerned him. A fair woman, not young but still attractive, and one who perhaps had been her lover in early youth, and might still hope, when she should become a richly-jointured widow, to secure her hand; and, by reason of his own successful schemes, the estate he surveyed daily with the complacency of a proprietor.

But pride, the bane of many a noble nature, kept the chief person concerned in the affairs of that falling house at a distance. Too truthful himself to doubt the word of another, Mackenzie believed whatever Muckle Colin's wife, who now seemed kind and tender, chose to tell him; and the period of his and Fraser's short leave of absence, which followed his recovery, wore away without his receiving the expected summons to visit his father.

His friend, meanwhile, made better use of the time which, on account of the exigencies of the war, he knew to be brief. Many a tryst had been held in Morag's fairy glen, many a love token exchanged, and many a promise spoken, before the lovers had courage to reveal their attachment.

After all, they needed not to fear. Mrs. Mackenzie was engaged with other thoughts, other combinations. The removal of one pair of quick, watchful, earnest eyes was a relief; for Morag, though not akin to him, dearly loved the old Laird, and she would have died to serve George, her adopted brother.

She had never been her mother's favourite. Donald was her pride and joy; and it was for him, and to conceal the effects of her own extravagance, that she was now struggling. It was very possible that the trusted ally, who was craftily dragging the old Laird's affairs into a web of legal subtleties, would in the end appropriate the lion's share, that she herself and her own son, as well as her stepson, might be left out in the cold—thus bringing retribution on her own head.

She was all smiles and sunshine when Fraser asked for the hand of her daughter. Morag might please herself, she said. If she were not afraid to be a soldier's wife in wartime, she had no opposition to dread. All she stipulated was that the marriage should take place at once, or not at all. She had a horror of long engagements.

It was not likely that a man passionately in love would object to this stipulation, but Morag hesitated. She and her lover were walking in the Beauly woods, when Fraser imparted to her the maternal verdict.

"Oh, I cannot!" the girl said, bursting into tears—"I cannot leave the poor old Laird."

"Nay, dearest; my claim is surely superior to his!" said Fraser reproachfully. "The Laird is not your father, he is not even related to you—he is only a connection by marriage. You will not give me up for his sake?"

Morag raised her eyes to his.

"I will wait patiently any number of years. You know that I will never marry another; but I am afraid to leave the old man entirely in the hands of my mother's kindred. I do not like her cousin, the Writer for the Signet, who comes down often from Edinburgh since her husband has been ill. He did not use to have him here. I think he is George and his father's bitter foe. There are wheels within wheels. I hear the whirr, but I cannot trace the pattern of the threads they are weaving."

"I think you are wrong in expressing such doubts of your mother," said Fraser gravely. "She seems to me to be devoted to her husband and is surely his proper guardian. Besides, what could you do to help or hinder? I would rather you were not mixed up in any way with conspiracies, if such exist in this house, contrary to its peace and honour."

Morag's slight form trembled with emotion.

"Do not blame me," she said softly. "My heart will go with you if I am left behind. But Donald is away. His studies will keep him at the University; and he will probably, when they are concluded, settle in the great city. He means to become a lawyer, on purpose to defend George's rights; but he is not a man yet. The time is far distant when he can be of use, and believe me, danger is much nearer—if not close at hand."

"These fear are visionary. You do not love me, Morag," said her angry lover. "Say at once that you are afraid to run the risks and encounter the difficulties of the wandering life we might share together—I think happily. Tell me the truth, and I will forgive it—bitter as that truth may be. You do not care enough for me to be willing to leave home and friends and country for my sake."

Morag turned away sorrowfully.

"I have few friends - none to compare with you and George. Since he and Donald left Redcastle, it has not seemed like home. I am no coward. It is cruel to doubt me."

"Forgive me, Morag. The disappointment has been very bitter of finding you alone unwilling to consent to my wish that you should become my wife. George was delighted when I confided in him, last night, the secret of our mutual attachment. He will be still more glad when he hears that by your mother's wish our marriage may take place at once, and that you can return with us to America. I had not expected opposition from you; but, I confess, the cordial agreement of your mother surprised while it charmed me."

"There is some motive for it, which we can none of us fathom," said Morag, doubtfully. "When you first paid me attention, she discouraged your suit."

"Perhaps she thought we were both of us too young to know our own minds?" said Fraser. "At all events, she favours my wooing now. You are the only doubter."

Their walk had brought them by this time to the spring in the woods, where George had slaked his thirst when first exiled from Redcastle. Fraser took the cup, and pledged his future bride, and Morag blushingly accepted his auguries of bliss.

As might be expected, her resolution did not hold out against her lover's and George's arguments, and her mother's fixed determination that the marriage must take place now, or never.

A very quiet party of family and friends and relatives met in the Chapel where the marriage of the young officer and Morag was solemnized a few weeks before the expiration of the time when he and Mackenzie must rejoin their regiment. The sea-voyage was then a much longer and more serious affair than it is now considered, and stirring events were anticipated. The mother-country had recognised that it was no playful game into which her rebellious children had entered, heart and soul, regardless of loss and human life.

All possible efforts on the part of the lovers of peace had been ineffectual. The Colonies refused to see that it was any part of their duty to assist in defraying expenses incurred without their consent; and the King was most reluctant to resign the fair Transatlantic jewels which adorned his crown.

Officers on leave were recalled to their war-like duty as hastily as in those days might be accomplished; a pressing summons reaching the brother-soldiers, now so closely connected by friendship, loyalty and affection, just at the time when Morag was hesitating as to the rival claims of duty. As usual, love gained the mastery.

The Laird was not present at the marriage. He was said by his wife to be more ailing than usual. Parting from Morag might be the reason, though she declared that he now seldom realized passing events. Morag herself said very little about their last interview. Her brother came from the Capital to give her away; and remained at the Castle until after the departure of the brother-officers and the young bride for the revolted Colonies.

George did not leave Scotland without a final effort to see his father. He had attended the marriage ceremony; though he refused to share in the feast which followed in the low, oak-panelled dining-room of "the oldest inhabited house in the country."While he awaited the return of the messenger he had sent to obtain permission to visit the Laird's apartments, he ran up to the ancient, low-browed, long, barrack-like room which he and Donald had occupied.

Tears sprang into his eyes as he looked at the flowers painted on the walls and the well-remembered devices which had been wrought by loving workmen many years before. He forgot his pride, his sense of injury, and would have given the whole world to hear his father's voice calling him, as it had often done in his boyhood, to share in some game or sport, by river, wood, and glen.

But it was not to be. On this side of the grave "Muckle Colin" and his soldier son were to meet no more. The young officer's face, pale from recent illness, flushed hotly when a message reached him, through the medium of a servant, forbidding any intrusion on his father's privacy. He had left home unbidden, and his return was not desired. He might drain the cup of malt, as he had brewed it.

The man stammered and blushed as he gave the rude reply to George's dutiful request. Those were the Laird's own words, he said; and he dared not disobey his master's orders, that they were to be repeated correctly.

From Morag the old Highland Chieftain took a much tenderer leave. He put into her hand a necklace of pearls, which had belonged to his first wife, and which he had managed to keep in his own possession; telling her that his blessing—the blessing of one to whom she had been like a daughter—went along with the gift.

Neither was her mother ungenerous at parting; though she often complained bitterly of narrow means. Many a patient-eyed Highland bull, many a silvery-fleeced sheep of the Redcastle estate, had perhaps passed into the hands of southern dealers to furnish Morag's tocher, which she believed to have been bequeathed to her by her own dead father. All these matters are wrapped in mystery, and can only form subjects for conjecture; or may be reports raised by prejudiced parties, who clung fondly to the ancient race from whom lands and gold were fast passing away.

CHAPTER XV.

Oh, the merry laughing comrade!
  Oh, the true and kindly friend!
Glowing hopes and lofty courage,
  Love and life, and thus they end!

Many a deed of valour brightened the closing cam-paigns of that bloody war; but, in spite of the un-exampled gallantry of an army which had in less than a year marched and counter-marched more than two thou-sand miles, fought several pitched battles, and endured unflinchingly every kind of suffering and privation, the days of British rule over the American colonies were num-bered.

Brave Charlie Campbell fell under a random shot at Fishing-Creek. It was he who commanded the light High-land companies which drove parts of Gates's army from a strong position near Campden to the cry "Remember you are Highlanders—Charge!" with such impetuosity that they were driven from the swampy plain like chaff before the wind.

A dread pause followed; the enemy then seemed to be gaining ground, and not perceiving through the smoke the fate of their companions gave cheers for victory as they took possession of the position evacuated by the Highlanders, who turned from pursuing their first opponents to fall upon them with such fury, that the majority threw down their arms and fled precipitately.

Colonel Macpherson of the 71st—Duncan of the Kiln, as he was called on account of his having been born in an old malt-kiln where his mother was forced to take refuge after the burning of her home, Cluny Castle—played an important part in the taking of Savannah. The kiln which sheltered his infancy never blazed more fiercely than the fire of battle along the causeway where he stood with the roar of the fight around him; while Baird, with his light infantry, rushed, under cover of the diversion he had made, through the swamp, and overpowered all resistance.

One of Macdonald's Highlanders, in the heat of the battle, rushed in front of a young officer of his own clan, saying:

"I promised faith to my King and to you, and neither bullet nor bayonet shall touch you, except through my body."

George Mackenzie and his brother-in-arms had their full share of fighting, and bore themselves well in camp and field. Morag followed as best she could the fortunes of the war, enduring bravely, with others of her sex, suspense, fatigue and hardship; and keeping as near to her husband and adopted brother as the regulations of the service permitted.

More than once the brother-officers saw the light of battle flash on the silver gorget as it rose above the dead and dying at Eutaw Creek and Parker's Ferry, Marion's first open field of pitched battle, where the splendid charge of Washington's cavalry broke the line of the flower of the British army.

Thanks to the Guerilla General, no more formidable force than Coffin's disabled cavalry hung on the rear of the American army after what they might well consider a victory at Eutaw Springs—the wild coralline-walled valley where Mackenzie and Fraser lost their way, and subsequently found shelter at the White House.

Never was the pellucid stream—purling through narrow fissures before it passes in many a curve and eddy to its underground passage and emerges again into daylight—so impeded in its shining course, as when, after the battle fought on its banks, on the 8th of September, 1781, by command of a British officer, the stocks of a thousand stand of arms were broken and thrown into the stream; and many of the brave fellows wounded by the swamp-fighters, in the impervious chaparral into which they had been beguiled, were left to fall into the enemy's hands.

In vain was all the valour previously displayed—useless the crushing defeat of Hampden and the capture of American guns. It was a victory gained by the rebels; and our dead left unburied in the swamp, our abandoned stores, lost for the King's army a prestige never to be regained.

The King of England "as well became him." A recent historian avers, though not specially responsible for the armed measures taken against the Colonists, "was the last to consent to the dismemberment of his dominions, the dishonour of his flag, and the abandonment of his loyal subjects, who had staked their property, their personal security, and even their lives on his cause."

It was, however, hopelessly lost when, judging his position in face of the united French and American army to be untenable, Cornwallis resolved to capitulate on the banks of the York river. The 71st Highlanders offered in vain to retake the redoubts captured by Washington and the Count de Rochambeau; and the British force, after an unsuccessful attempt to remove the elite of the army and leave a small force to capitulate—which was frustrated by a squall of wind—marched out with arms and baggage, October 8, 1781.

Morag enjoyed the sad privilege of nursing her husband, who had been severely wounded at the battle near Eutaw Creek. After he was pronounced out of danger by the military surgeon, Fraser was removed, at the Chevalier's express desire, to the White House, which was still a sacred refuge for the sick and weary. Clara found consolation for her own grief in helping the young wife to nurse her husband, who was still her lover. As Mackenzie had prophesied, she did not hate the rushing river, though its song reminded her always of that terrible night in flood-time.

She was, though no vows passed her lips, devoted to the task of consoling the afflicted, and ministering to the sick sufferers daily brought within these hospitable gates. Sometimes it might be a rebel soldier, sometimes a loyalist. At others a peasant or and Indian, or a poor way-farer. It mattered not which: all were alike received and kindly treated so long as their need lasted.

The tide of war was stayed, but the evils it had brought in its train lasted long; and the whole country, devastated by tramp of horses, incendiary fires, pestilence and scarcity, was in a miserably unsettled state.

As soon as the claims of duty permitted, George Mackenzie made his way to Casa Bianca. He found its inmates in a state of great agitation, in consequence of the resolution formed by the revered head of the family to return to his native country. The ungrateful persecution to which the great Portuguese Minister was subjected by the daughter of the Monarch he had so faithfully served for the best part of his life excited the Chavalier's just indignation.

"A set of crazy devotees!" he exclaimed, disrespectfully alluding to Doña Maria and her Court. "What is the benefit of their pretended piety—their daily masses and rhapsodies—if they are to undo all the good that years of reform and energetic administration have effected for my unhappy country? Of what can the new Queen accuse her faithful servant? Not of avarice; for he has received barely a hundred a year of your English money in addition to his salary as Secretary of State. Not one of the customary gratuities bestowed by sovereigns on those who serve them faithfully, has sullied his hands."

Tears stood in the old nobleman's eyes as he recalled the difference in the state of the kingdom as he had seen it when Lisbon lay in ruins after the earthquake, and her fairest provinces impoverished and desolate, to what it had become under Pombal and the good King Joseph's fostering care.

"Look at the waving fields of grain, where once stunted vineyards yielded only sour wine, the soil being unfitted for grape culture. I can remember the outcry against the decree of the 26th of October, 1765, which directed that within the space of three months, in certain districts, the vines should be rooted up, and the land sewn with corn. What a commotion ensued; but how wise was the decision! In the Northern Provinces, on the contrary, the best means were employed to encourage vine-culture; and while the open country on either side of the Tagus, the Mondego, and the Sacavem, and the great plains were yellow with corn which supported the population, the banks of the rivers not suitable for arable purposes were planted with rows of shadowing trees.

"What a man he was! Nothing escaped him! Look at the splendid educational establishments founded by him, alike for the children of the nobility, and the poorest peasant. See our noble Universities and public Institutions restored and reformed; - Arts and Sciences flourishing, men of letters encouraged; commerce protected, yet unfettered by unwise restrictions, gold pouring into the mother-country from our Colonies: our national credit re-established. And this man, the saviour of his country—now that four-score honourable years have passed over his venerable head, is reduced to the humiliation of a degrading scrutiny into the labours of a life devoted to his sovereign, and to his fellow-creatures!"

The Chevalier paused, choked by emotion.

"I cannot leave him to suffer alone. Perhaps my evidence may be useful; and the repeal of all the sentences passed on every member of the Tavora family, however little they could be suspected of complicity in the conspiracy, removes all difficulties out of my road. Perhaps the Queen and her Consort may yet listen to reason. At all events I cannot remain idle. I must be on the spot to vindicate the greatest minister Portugal—perhaps any country—has ever gloried in, from false accusations."

Mackenzie inquired whether the ladies of the family would accompany the Chevalier.

"No, no; by no means. I shall not at present, take them to that priest-ridden Court," said the Doctor. "Clara and Rozay are good girls, good Christians as my wife has ever been; - good Catholics, also like myself, though my enemies call me a heretic. I never abjured, or wished to alter, the form of worship in which my excellent parents brought me up, nor would I for worlds disturb their convictions. It is bigotry which I dislike—above all Jesuitry—

as my great master, Pombal, did before me. His influence, and that of the good and great Pope, banished the Jesuits from the Courts of Europe; but I fear they are now creeping in at all points—to our homes, our councils, our seminaries. Here we are free from them; and, if I take the women of my house away from America, it will be to England probably, but not yet a while. At Casa Bianca I can leave them without fear."

Emboldened by his liberal sentiments George said, abruptly:

"Senhor, will you give me Rozay, your ward, for my wife? I might be of some use as a protector to the ladies of your family during your absence. I, too, am a good Catholic Christian, though the Priests would call me a heretic. I do not think we would ever disagree about religious matters; and we love each other dearly!"

The Chevalier looked gravely, but not unkindly, at the young officer, whose fair face was suffused with blushes.

"So you have stolen a march upon me! I had not thought of this. Rozay is my child, as well as my ward. She and Clara have always been—will always be—treated as sisters. Since the day when by our hasty flight, Rozay was involved in our wandering fortunes, the little gypsy has been dear to me as a daughter. What provision can you make for her future welfare, or for her children, if they be granted to you? I am afraid you are too young and thoughtless to undertake the cares of a father of a family."

"Try me!" said Mackenzie, earnestly. "Though not hith-erto one of Fortune's favourites, adversity has not been without its sweet uses to me. Above all, it has taught me trust in Providence, and self-reliance."

"I believe you have profited by the hard schooling and severe discipline to which you have patiently submitted," said the old nobleman, eyeing him observantly. "I have heard a good deal about you from your friend, who is a right good fellow, while I suppose you were stealing my pretty Rozay's heart away from us all. But you must have a home to take her to, before I give my consent to the mar-riage; and you are both too young. Let it rest until my re-turn from Portugal."

Mackenzie was well satisfied with his partial success. He had scarcely hoped more than not to be prohibited from prosecuting his suit. There were tokens of kindly re-gard in the Chevalier's voice and manner which made him augur well for the ultimate success of his wooing. Many an evening on the banks of the broad river were spent by the happy lovers in planning for the future; when the young heir of Redcastle might take his bride to the old red-sandstone Castle on the shore of the Moray Firth.

CHAPTER XVI.

We were nothing but children, then, darling;
  Our love but a species of play;
But my heart was sore when he left me,
  And I thought of him night and day.

I made him a purse for his money, dear,
  Alas, 'twas a scanty store! -
A sixpence we broke between us—
  Some coins—hardly more than a score.

He had that which no wealth can buy, darling,
  Bright truth and an honest hand;
With the deep first love of a faithful heart,
  Which absence could well withstand.

R. M. K.

The Scottish youth spoke only the truth when he assured Rozay Morais' kind, fatherly guardian that they were not likely to quarrel about their religion. Though brought up to use different forms of worship, and not inclined to change, the spirit of love and charity inflamed the hearts of both the young lovers; and on less essential points than the earnest Christian's faith and hope, they could wisely agree to differ.

In the Chevalier's household his word was law, subject only to the will of a heavenly Father; and his orders were always in accordance with Divine command. Clara and Rozay obeyed implicitly one whom each regarded as a parent; and they worshipped as he did, after the fashion of their forefathers. It was a simple faith, full of reverence, combining spiritual with earthly duty. The Roman father was never more completely the leader of his own family worship—the sustainer of the sacred fire on the domestic altar—than the cultivated Lusitanian noble.

The priest who was to have officiated at Clara's uncompleted bridal was the friend and adviser of the whole household; but confessions of their small venial errors were made by the young girls to their parents and to their God, in the sacred privacy of home.

In a free country, the liberality of the Chevalier's opinions had not exposed him or his family to persecution or misconstruction, but he was probably right in judging it best to preserve his family from the influence of the priest-ridden court which had succeeded good King Joseph's liberal and intellectual circle.

The new Queen had shown more respect for a somewhat doubtful construction of her royal father's last wishes, than for his transparently clear direction that his friend and faithful minister should continue to enjoy his well-earned honours. It was but natural that at the moment of death the good King should wish to extend that mercy to others which he himself hoped to receive; but the unseemly haste with which the conspirators against her father's life were suddenly released did not meet with

Pombal's approval, and was said not to have been fully resolved upon by the dying monarch.

Pombal's resignation of office had been gladly accepted—the salary he had received as secretary-of-state,
conferred on him for life, - the Commandery of St. Jago
de Lanhozo being added as an especial mark of honour,
in consequence of the high and singular esteem which the
Queen's father had entertained for him—but these early
tokens of favour were only temporary.

The act of clemency which released so many dangerous
state-criminals, led to the prosecution of the vigilant minister who had detected their treason. The ecclesiastics,
who now carried all before them, were Pombal's sworn
foes; and, under their influence, most of the wise reforms
and regulations Don Joseph and his minister had inaugurated, were speedily abolished.

Superstition and gloom took the place of gaiety and re-
fined intellectual amusements in the beautiful capital.
The excellent opera company formed by Don Joseph
ceased to afford entertainment to the Queen, whose weak-
ened intellect was unable to withstand the fanatical ex-
hortations of her priestly advisers. Respect for the
memory of her father did not prevent Doña Maria's attending to the counsels of the ambitious and designing
nobles and ecclesiastics who surrounded her; nor en-
lighten her understanding to perceive that the cruelly false
accusations against his tried and trusted minister, reflected discredit on the master as well as the servant.

A great friendship sprang up beside the young Highland officer's bed of suffering, between his wife and Clara. Fraser's severe wound had not healed speedily. It was to be feared that his military career was closed. At the best, a long period of inactivity must be endured. Under these circumstances an arrangement was made that, during the Chevalier's visit to Europe, Morag and her husband should reside at Casa Bianca, where George Mackenzie could occasionally visit them.

Though there was no formal engagement, the attachment between Rozay and her Highland laddie had received the sanction of her guardian's silent approval. The Chevalier, with his keen but kindly glance, could read the open brow, and even see into the honest heart of the Scotchman. Fraser had told him the story of his sufferings in his early home, and also the exemplary conduct which had redeemed the rashness of his enlistment. While prudence enjoined delay, hope was not prohibited; and opportunities were allowed the young couple to become better known to each other.

The happiness of others did not sadden the unselfish girl, widowed even before her bridal. Morag, in spite of much anxiety, was happy, and daily and hourly rejoiced in being privileged to attend on her wounded hero. The sight of her devotion and its reward was no more painful to Clara than the song of the river, whose rapid rush had seemed to bear to her ears her lover's dying call.

Never was that voice silent. It echoed in the plaintive

sweep of the water through the bulrushes, in the cry of the wild birds swooping over the osier-beds, in the monotonous song of the whip-poor-will, and in the roar of the flood. Yet she still loved the broad bright stream which had carried away the hopes of her young life; and still, while she had a heart which beat responsively to every tone of human suffering, there were chords which rang clearly out in sympathy with human love and youthful joy.

Although Mackenzie had borne the perils of war better than his brother-in-arms, they had left their mark. The passage of the spent ball across his broad chest often caused severe pain, and had inflicted an ineffaceable scar; a faint trace of which reappeared on the white bosom of our own mother, his eldest child, and remained there till her death. He had lost much of his gay spirits, not only during the sorrowful banishment from his Highland home, but from sad experience of mortal conflict. The old trees by the Strath, the rosy walls of the Red Castle of his ancestors, might greet him, should he revisit Scotland, with the refrain:

> "You have looked upon death since we met you
> last."

But there were hours when Mackenzie's eyes would flash with their own light, and his cheeks glow—when pain and regret would be banished—as he stood by Rozay's side on the river bank, her hand in his, her voice sounding with marvellous sweetness in his ears. Though not al-

lowed all the privileges of engaged lovers, though in obedience to what he knew were her guardian's wishes,
Mackenzie said little about the love which filled his heart
and gleamed in his blue eyes, George knew that the girl
by his side was as much his own as if bound by a thousand
troth-plights.

There were moments when they were alone, for
Madame loved them both, and was not a vigilant or sus-
picious chaperon. She trusted in his honour and she was
not deceived. George did not sully the girl's ears with flat-
teries, or presume upon her love. Without caresses, without subtlety, he wooed her with the homage of a true and
reverent affection. The birds overhead, the waters flowing
past their feet, the twinkling stars and silver moon, were
not more clear and pure than those love-dreams.

Active warfare had ceased, though the preliminaries of
peace were not sufficiently settled for the British troops to
be withdrawn from her self-emancipated colonies. In consideration of the delicacy of her health, and through the
kindness of his commanding officer, Mackenzie was en-
abled to pass much of his time in the house which seemed
more like home to him than his birthplace.

When in camp he carried with him, and found in them
a panacea for all evils and misgivings, the half coin he had
broken, and given its counterpart to Rozay on Savannah's
bank, and the little purse she had knitted for him as they
sat in the vine-roofed arbour where he had first breathed
his love-tale in her modest ears, and seen that bright blush

mantle on her cheek which inspires hope.

Mackenzie, though often much absorbed, never neglected the calls and requirements of duty. He was, first of
all, a British officer; and though he hoped the war was
over, there was much to be done in the regiment. He ex-
erted himself not only to preserve good discipline among
his former colleagues, the privates and non-commissioned
officers, but to keep them in health and spirits, encour-
aging hardy games and exercises and every kind of whole-
some recreation.

All his men adored him, excepting those whom neither
kindness nor justice could touch and tame. With them,
and with them only, he was severe. Though grave beyond
his years he had plenty of sympathy with youthful error;
and many a casual offender looked back with gratitude,
in after life, to the officer who had taken the trouble to
explain to him that the path of duty and of sobriety led
straight to honour and promotion; and was, though difficult at the outset, easiest, if stedfastly pursued.

The man who spoke had known and experienced their
trials, and could therefore deal with them authoritatively.
He had, too, a firm faith in the one great leader of armies,
in the one Saviour of sinners. Those who cared for serious
thoughts, those who desired aid and instruction in grap-
pling with the obstructions which are nowhere more dis-
heartening than in a soldier's career, knew that a lamp
burned nightly in his quarters, and that, by its light, the
young officer was willing to read and explain to those who

cared to listen, that word of God by which his own footsteps were guided.

CHAPTER XVII.

"The wild south sweeps the bay,
    The stars come overhead;
Gone is the fair-eyed day,
    That and my love are dead.

"The ravening sea-fowls scream
    O'er the black-ribbed ocean bed,
Its waters are fed like a dream,
    That and my love are dead.

"The sand-rose lies at my feet
    Dark matted where it spread
Like flame, running blossoming sweet,-
    It and my love are dead.

"No, no; love never dies;
    Some day will be falsely said
When low this mortal lies,
    Life and her love are dead."

SONGS OF ERSKINELAND.

As the Chevalier's beautiful daughter wandered on the river's bank, often sad and solitary, with the beautiful luxuriant vegetation and unnumbered flowers of that rich moist soil blooming around her, life at times seemed to stretch before her into a dreary waste. The song of the waters sounded like her young lover's dirge, and the glories of earth, sea, and sky seemed a mockery of her grief.

But it is well to bear the yoke in our youth, as George Mackenzie had testified. There are moments when the impatient soul longs to free itself; and there are others, solemn and still, when it recognises the hand which, even while laying on the burden, gives strength to bear it; and then, after the struggle is over, there is peace. Nothing, after that fierce pang, after that heartbreak—nothing can wound us in that way more! We submit, and, in submitting, we find that after the storm comes sunshine, - if not the gleam of noonday, the tranquil, blessed twilight—the repose of early morning and late evening.

No one would have called Clara unhappy. She was ready to sympathize in the joys as well as the sorrows all around—perhaps seeking most of all the society of the young and the happy.

Rozay found in her an untiring listener, and Clara acquiesced in all her plans for the future, during which they were never to be separated. Did she remember—could she ever forget—her own and Philip Lavigne's visions of bliss, in which, too, her sister-cousin always had a share? No; she recalled them faithfully; it was not her nature to forget: but even as she still found pleasure in arranging the flowers and culling the fruit which she and Rozay had prepared, with songs on their innocent lips, for her own bridal feast, so she now enjoyed, vicariously, the love-dreams and Paradisaical fancies of those whose life-path lay bright in the sunshine before them.

No terrors about that distant country, with its stern grey mountain and rough moorland, dark fir-forests, and long cold winters, which sometimes frightened Rozay, darkened Clara's spirit. All climes, all seasons could be endured in company with those we love. The same heaven on which her hopes rested would gleam above the Scottish Highlands in paler blue, flecked with dimmer stars, and less brilliant moonlight, as she now looked up to, hopefully, by day and night on Savannah's bank—deep in colour, glowing in warm radiance. The same great God ruled over all.

Fraser's wound was healing now, under the care of his devoted nurses; and he loved to sit in the arbour on the river-bank, and watch the flow of the stream, with Morag and Clara reading to him and waiting upon him. Madame would bring her beautiful delicate embroidery - the art she had learnt in her convent school—and sit quietly, apparently listening; but often her thoughts wandered off to her native land—to him who was still her lover after many years of wedlock, and who was faithfully watching over the declining months of the great Minister whose sun was setting in the darkness of unmerited persecution.

In the little retired town which bore his name, Pombal lived quietly and contentedly, until the malice of his enemies invaded even this humble retreat.

"Like Sully," he often said, "I can live more happily in retirement than in the grandeur of a Court. You see this humble cabin, - it is not mine—I have hired it. The man who is accused of consulting his own interests has not even built himself a cottage in his native place. They allowed me to bring my books, and I desire little else."

His chief effort was to console the Marchioness, who felt the change in their fortunes more than himself. The Chevalier said she still preserved her great beauty, and was always attired with taste. Their children, from time to time, visited them; but the solitude, after a life spent in the great world, was very trying to the noble Austrian lady, a niece of the great Marshal Daun, to whom Maria Theresa considered she owed the preservation of her throne.

Often the poor lady could not restrain her tears when the sight of an old friend of former days, like the Chevalier de Lucena, and other circumstances, reminded her of the greatness of their fall.

"She has the pride of her nation," the Chevalier added, in the graphic account he wrote to his wife of the visit to his old friend; "and cannot forget all the tributes once paid to her husband's merits. 'It is but natural,' the Marquis said to me. 'To console her is my chief desire and occupation. By following my example she will soon learn to support our affliction.'"

"Their 'hermit's frugal repast,' as the Marquis called it, was well served without ostentation; and bread and broth were distributed, afterwards, to two hundred poor people.

"In the evenings Pombal was usually immersed in his books, but he found time to continue the conversation into which he had entered at the dinner-table.

"'The Portuguese people cannot hate me,' he said with emotion. 'It is impossible for every reason. What is a Portuguese now, and what was he forty years ago? Was it not I who made him feel his independence? Have I not established, throughout the country, education, manufactures, and the arts? Did I not rebuild nearly a third of the city of Lisbon? Was not industry, with its attendant prosperity, roused to the greatest activity during my administration? Impossible! Considering all the claims I have to the gratitude of the people, I believe them too just to wish my injury. I will tell you who are the authors of all you may have seen and heard in the Capital. Those of the nobility whose insolent pretensions I destroyed are using every endeavour to compass my ruin. They cannot with decency show themselves at the head of the persecuting party, so they have selected some of their creatures, who, disguised as barbers, sailors, servants, and such like, frequent the public places, abusing me, and painting me in the most odious colours.

"'Look yonder,' he added, pointing to a large building; 'that is a warehouse belonging to the town. I built it as a public granary, and it is full of corn.'

"He stopped abruptly, and there were tears in my eyes as well as his; we were both thinking, I have no doubt, of the same thing.

"Certainly my reflections had gone back to the past, - to the days of our youth, when the fields lay fallow, or totally destitute of culture; when the natural resources of our native land were utterly neglected; when Portugal, which formerly had exported corn, was dependent on foreign nations for that first necessary of existence.

"Pombal's wise decrees were not, as was falsely affirmed, new crotchets; they enforced old laws, evaded by the proprietors of the land. Walled quintas, heights and declivities, where the vine could flourish, were exempted from their operation. In places which produced only a sour, unprofitable vintage, an abundant harvest was substituted."

Clara's dark eyes flashed with enthusiasm as she read aloud, with her mother's permission, the Chevalier's interesting letter to those assembled in the vine-arbour. All her earliest memories—all her most cherished associations—were linked with her father's friend, the great Minister now in retirement.

"Ah, poor lady!" said Madame; "it is hardest for her! M. de Pombal has the relief of rest after toil. He has his books and his own great thoughts to console him. Women suffer most from these terrible reverses. They hear and know all the gossip—the insinuations—which they loyally keep from the ears of their husbands. The Marquis is a philosopher, and, what is more, a good Christian; but he cannot hide from the wife of his bosom how much he suffers from the Queen's ingratitude. Respect for her father's memory should have prevented her assenting to measures which reflect on him, as well as on his faithful adviser. But she has surrendered her conscience into the hands of unscrupulous men, who were, and are, the Marquis's bitter foes. Read, my good Clara, her last public decree, in which the greatest statesman of the age is treated like a culprit."

"And yet, after the keenest investigation, no evidence has been found against him," said Clara indignantly, after reading with a trembling voice the cruel document, in which, under a pretence of clemency, the complete refutation of all charges against him, proffered by the Marquis, was consigned to oblivion, and stigmatized as an appeal for forgivenesss.

"Our hero will not say, like the great English Cardinal, 'If I had served my God as I have served my King, He would not have deserted me in my old age,'" added Clara. "No; our great Minister served God and the King; and he will bear patiently the will of his Heavenly Master. Oh, I can fancy him, like the great Apostle, dwelling in his hired house, beloved by all good men! Mother, we must not urge my father to leave him. Let him have one faithful friend near him in adversity. He who was surrounded by troops of flatterers, now needs the faithful service he performed till death to his own royal friend and master!"

Madame was silent; but her daughter's words were not unheeded. Mother and daughter were alike in their noble unselfishness.

PART THE FOURTH.

"The sunbeams lost for half a year
    Slant through my pane their morning rays;
For dry North-westers, cold and clear
    The East blows in its thin blue haze.

"The golden-chaliced crocus burns;
    The long narcissus-blades appear;
The cone-beaked hyacinth returns
    And lights her blue-flamed chandelier.

"The willows' whistling lashes, wrung
    By the wild winds of gusty March,
With sallow leaflets lightly strung
    Are swaying by the tufted larch.

"When wake the violets, Winter dies;
    When sprout the elm-buds, Spring is near;
When lilac blossoms, Summer cries,
    Bud, little roses! Spring is here!

"Wild filly from the mountain-side
    Doomed to the close and clasping thrills,
Lend me thy long untiring stride
    To seek with thee thy western hills."

OLIVER WENDELL HOLMES.

CHAPTER XVIII.

"Round the sylvan fairy nooks
    Feathery brackens fringe the rocks,
'Neath the brae the burnie jouks,
    And ilka thing is cheerie, O!
Trees may bud, and birds may sing,
    Flowers may bloom and verdure spring,
Joy to me they canna bring
    Unless wi' thee, my dearie, O!'

TANNAHILL.

Autumn had glowed in the American forests, Winter had passed away, and the early Spring had come, without bringing the Chevalier back to his Transatlantic home. The women of his household had been true to his trust, had borne themselves wisely and well, and had not clamoured for the return of their natural protector.

Now they were rewarded for their forbearance. Madame's faded cheek flushed like a girl's with happiness, when her husband hinted at the possibility of their returning to Portugal. There was a change in the tone of his last letters. He was hoping for better things—for the renewal of prosperity; and he was not the man to draw back if it were likely that he might aid in the restoration of national improvements which, in past years, had been partly his work, under the leading of the great Minister.

He had been summoned by the Queen and her consort the Infante, always an upright, clear-sighted guide to Doña Maria, when she listened to his counsels in preference to her priestly advisers, and had been offered a place in the new Cabinet. The friendship he had shown to the Marquis was not reckoned to his discredit. On the contrary, it seemed to have won for him courtly favour.

Some lingering womanly emotions had been stirred in Doña Maria's heart by the report of the Chevalier's faithfulness to the unfortunate nobleman; and, as a child, she had been very fond of him. In a private interview she spoke feelingly about Pombal and her father, acknowledging that during his lifetime the Marquis had served him and the country well. Then, abruptly dismissing the topic, she reverted to the pardon of all who were supposed to have been inculpated in the great conspiracy.

It was but fair, she said, that the Chevalier should share in this amnesty. Neither she nor the Infante believed him to have been even an accessory to the crime, though, at the time, it was difficult to separate the innocent from the guilty. All who survived had suffered long enough. Her father in his last hours had enjoined leniency.

It was the Queen's intention now, as she graciously intimated, to restore all his forfeited honours and estates to the Chevalier, and to add to their number. It was also her express desire that Madame and her beautiful daughter, should return to their palace in Lisbon, where she herself and Don Pedro had passed many happy hours; and become members and ornaments of her courtly circle.

The Chevalier could not fail to be deeply flattered by his reception, and retired from the royal presence convinced of his Sovereign's sincerity. The invitation to bring back his family was, in point of fact, a command which he felt it incumbent upon him to obey. He had accepted office, and hoped it might be in his power to modify the harsh measures lately promulgated against the Marquis de Pombal; who did not wish to return to Court or the Capital, but trusted that his declining years might be allowed to pass away tranquilly in his native town.

George Mackenzie, who was staying at Casa Bianca when this letter arrived, listened to its contents with consternation.

"Is Rozay to be taken away from me?" he continued. "Will you carry her among those priests and courtiers who will persuade her that her own Hieland laddie is a heretic, and will steal her away from me? Madame, I have been patient hitherto, but this I cannot bear. Will you not plead for us?"

Rozay, too, looked very sad, though she had no misgivings respecting her own constancy. Both the young lovers wrote to the Chevalier. Madame and Clara pleaded warmly in their behalf.

Nearly a year had passed since their attachment had received, at least, tacit approval. They both declared themselves to be much older and wiser, and quite competent to decide what would best secure their future happiness in life. They reminded the Chevalier that he had promised to take the matter into consideration on his return. If he was not coming back to Casa Bianca, now that the stamp of time was set upon their love, might it not be sanctified by marriage?

After some delay, during which George rejoined his regiment, now encamped near Augusta, an answer was received favourable to his wishes. The Chevalier approved highly of all that he had been told him of his conduct lately, as well as of what he had himself witnessed. If Madame cordially agreed with the measure, and could undertake, in addition to her own responsibilities, the trouble it would involve, permission was given by Rozay's Guardian for the celebration of their marriage, previous to her departure for Lisbon.

Madame joyfully gave her consent, and preparations were immediately set on foot. She wisely decided that George and Rozay should not be married at Casa Bianca. The association with Clara's contemplated espousals would be too painful for any of them to bear.

The additional responsibility she accepted willingly. An efficient ally to aid her in her exertions had sprung up unexpectedly in the person of her son, long absent in the Brazils. He had come to aid her and her sister in their preparations for departure, and to escort them home. It was from him, as the representative of his father, that the

Scottish youth was to receive the hand of Rozay Morais.

Honourably engaged in the diplomatic service of his country, and occupied with the care of his father's property in the Brazils, the young Chevalier had seen very little of his mother and sister since his boyhood. They now rejoiced at the reunion, after long separation. The beautiful girl who bore so bravely her load of sorrow, found it lightened by the love and sympathy of her brother.

Clara was the most reluctant to leave Casa Bianca; and her kind mother yielded to her wish to linger among the scenes she loved till the last moment. She was thus spared the sight of preparations similar to those which in her own case had proved unavailing, and which must have reawakened sad memories.

Alone, or with her brother, she wandered by the river, or sat in the vine-wreathed arbour; sometimes listening to marvellous tales about the diamond and ruby mines—at others, absorbed in thought, watching the young Spring foliage quivering in the sunlight, with rays darting through trellis and leaf, or falling on the river as it glided swiftly past.

The brother and sister were together in the arbour towards the close of a warm day, Madame and Rozay being absent on an expedition to the city, when footsteps were heard approaching; not swift and light, like the Indian tread, but sounding weary and heavy.

"It is some poor traveller," said Clara, putting aside a screening bough, with fearlessness and kindly hospitality, for which the place was famous. "Let us give him a welcome to needful rest."

Her brother, not yet accustomed to the ways of his father's house, was inclined to use more caution.

"In these war-times, when men are tramping about the country, it is well to know what kind of guest we are admitting. This may not be a solitary harmless wayfarer."

He rose and went a few steps along the path by the river-side, to meet the stranger. A fair-haired, long-legged Scotch youth, with a dusty plaid about his shoulders, confronted him.

"Is there one who calls himself George Mackenzie, the Master of Redcastle, in yonder white house?" he said. "I have come a long way, and across the sea, to have speech with him."

"It is Donald!" said Clara pleasantly, coming out of the arbour with extended hand, while her brother, somewhat perplexed, stood back. "You are very like your sister. I should have known, too, by your voice only, that you were Morag's brother. Oh, how tired you must be! Come to the house, and rest and refresh yourself before we ask or answer any questions except the one just spoken, and another which I guess to be on your lips. You have come to the right place, and all is well with Morag, and George Mackenzie."

Donald yielded as readily to her welcome suggestion as he might to the guidance of an angel. In her cool white dress he thought that the lady looked like one, as she led him by the hand to the wide veranda, where, speedily, iced drinks, fruits, cakes and sweet-meats were placed before him.

A more solid repast, Clara told him, would be ready by the time he had enjoyed his bath and siesta. Meanwhile she would go and see after the arrangements necessary for preparing a room for his occupation, and send Morag to welcome him.

With unpractised gallantry Donald kissed the fair hand he was about to relinquish, before Clara left him. He then, with boyish alacrity, which his law-studies in Edinburgh had not destroyed, attacked the light viands and refreshing beverages on the stand in front of the couch on which he had thrown himself. He thought of the tales he had read and heard in his childhood, and recognised in the houri who had quitted him one gifted with that spirit of true Oriental hospitality which forbids the harassed, wayworn guest to be tormented with questions until his bodily wants are supplied.

Morag's light, hurrying footsteps roused her brother from the reverie into which he had fallen. It was a sufficient reward for all he had undergone during his rapid journey—undertaken on the impulse of the moment with but scanty resources—to feel his sister's warm tears and kisses on his cheeks, and to receive Fraser's hearty greeting.

He could not help wishing, nevertheless, to see again the ministering angel who was providing invisibly for his reception. He was much too tired, he said, to tell them what had brought him across the seas until he had been refreshed, as she had suggested, with a bath and siesta, and shaken the dust from his travelling garb.

The large, cool room, with its closely-drawn jalousies and open windows, delighted the weary guest. Outside, the water gurgled among the bulrushes, and the leaves of the high trees rustled in the land-breeze.

After his bath, Donald lay resting, not asleep, but dreaming of a dark-haired, dark-eyed maiden, with sweet smiles, greeting him on the river-bank, recognising the wandering laddie far frae hame and his ain dear countrie—that north countrie, so dear to the Highlander. At last the vision faded; sweet, untroubled repose fell upon the youth's weary eyelids.

When he awoke, the soft spring dusk, which lasts so short a time in those climes, compared to its length in the British Isles, filled the room. Donald started up and dressed himself hastily. He felt quite ready for the substantial meal promised by the houri, and still more anxious for her gracious presence.

The whole family were assembled in the veranda when he found his way back to it. George greeted him with a brother's warmth. It seemed quite an understood thing that he should take his place amongst them unquestioned. He was introduced to Rozay, and guessed, when he saw her blushes and George's proud glance, in what relation they stood to each other.

George had returned from the city with Madame and his betrothed. It had been a great surprise to hear of Donald's arrival—a surprise mingled with pleasure, when he thought how true a friend he should have to stand beside him at the altar.

Again Donald put aside all questioning. It would be time enough to tell on the morrow all he knew, and did not know, about Redcastle. He had not been there lately, but he had seen his mother. When she left home there was no great change there.

The boy had become a man, George saw, and he had the discretion of manhood. Not another syllable could be extracted from him. On other subjects he could talk, and talk well. The incidents of the voyage and long journey, all its perils and adventures, were lightly and amusingly told, and, in the genial society he had fallen into so easily, fatigue was forgotten.

Rozay touched her guitar, and soothed his senses with sweet melody. He longed to hear Clara sing; but as far as music was concerned, her voice had been silent since the time when that wild call came across the water to her ear alone. Something in her manner, though he was unacquainted with her sad history, prevented the words passing his lips, with which he was about to ask her to take up the graceful instrument which her cousin had laid down.

Madame felt a motherly kindness for the youth who was far from his home, and treated him like one of the family. Morag and her husband were delighted to be with him, and told him, without waiting to be asked, their plans for the future.

Several of the British officers had received grants of land in the newly-settled Colonies. Among the rest, Major Fraser, whose severe wound incapacitated him for active service in other parts of the world, meant to make his home in New Brunswick.

They were as full of plans for leading the life of settlers in the woods, as Morag and her brother had often been in childhood, when they played beside the Moray Firth and fancied it like the broad Atlantic.

Donald fell asleep at last, with the sound of the American river in his ears, mingling with the voices of his home, but seeming yet sweeter in this strange land and after long absence.

CHAPTER XIX.

"Loveliest of lovely things are they,
      On earth, that soonest pass away.
The rose that lives its little hour
      Is prized beyond the sculptured flower;
Even love, long tried and cherish'd long,
      Becomes more tender and more strong,
At thoughts of that insatiate grave
      From which its yearnings cannot save.
"River! in this still hour thou hast
      Too much of heaven on earth to last;
Not long may thy still waters lie,
      An image of the glorious sky.
Thy fate and mine are not repose;
      And, ere another evening close,
Thou to thy tides shalt turn again,
      And I to seek the crowd of men."

WILLIAM CULLEN BRYANT.

To the Highland youth, lately condemned to pass his time in a lawyer's office, that fair American river and the white-walled compound, the vine-wreathed walls of Casa Bianca, with the dark-eyed woman who graced its chambers or strolled along the flower-enamelled mead, appeared like Paradise.

Donald was up and abroad in the early morning, tasting the fragrance of the new-born day. He was returning from a long solitary ramble on the river's bank, when he encountered Clara coming forth from the house, with a basket on her arm. She was tenderly supporting a chaplet of white flowers, which rested partly against the side of the light wicker framework, partly against her slender fingers, and neither invited nor prohibited the youth's attendance, but she silently negatived his offer to relieve her of her slight burden. Something in the sad, graceful gesture prevented its repetition, but they walked together towards the labourers' huts, sheltered by a group of trees, which were clustered within the walls of the compound.

Clara did not cross the allotment-ground belonging to the cottages, or enter any of the humble dwellings, which, on other occasions, she frequently visited; but turned off by a little path to a white-walled simple edifice where the services of the Church were held. There were only a few graves scattered round it. Donald stood back when he guessed her intention, but he watched her slight figure as she moved onward, and saw her place the wreath on a green hillock which was marked by a marble cross.

He could not see the inscription, but concluded one of the family was buried there. When Clara returned to his side, after removing a faded garland and a few withered leaves, her face was calm but very pale. She said nothing about her sad errand, but he noticed that she carried with her the relics of the flowers which she had replaced with fresher emblems of affection, as though even when withered they were precious.

"We shall not be long at Casa Bianca," she said, as they retraced their steps. "I shall be very sorry to leave our home in the wilderness. There are no associations for me like those that bind my mother's heart to Portugal; her native land, the scene of her early life, and of many happy years."

"You will be sorely missed here, "said the youth, who had heard blessings murmured as they passed the men's gardens, and seen the children run out to meet his beautiful companion. "What will become of this settlement when you all return to Europe?"

"My father has made arrangements," said Clara, gravely. "He never overlooks any duty. Besides, he says we may return. He is not at all sure of remaining at Court. Meanwhile the good Padre will look after our poor people, and minister to the wants of wayfarers and outcasts. Hospitality is often needed her."

"A man might be worse off than at Casa Bianca," said Donald, somewhat abruptly. "If Don Diego should want an agent here, I wish he would give me the chance. I don't think I shall stop long at home. When George has his rights I shall go and seek my fortune, and a fairer spot than this could not easily be found. Will you let me lay a flower on your little brother or sister's grave for you in that case?"

A faint blush rose up in Clara's cheek.

"I thought you knew," she said falteringly. "It is not a brother or a sister's grave that is under the shadow of those trees. One who was even dearer to me than they could have been, lost his life in crossing yonder river when it was in flood, to come to me."

Donald's heart stood still. He could find no words in which to ask pardon for his indiscretion; and so, as doubtless was best, he kept silence.

"Do not grieve for me," said Clara, gently; "no words can add to, or lessen, my life-long grief. Nor can that silent marble reveal what times I have visited this spot, or been absent from it. In the days to come, my feet may never return to it; who can guess the future? But wherever I may be, my thoughts will fly here, and I fancy there is a communion of thought between the dead and living. Philip will know that he is not forgotten."

A dream seemed dispelled by her soft words—by her truthful accents. Donald did not repeat his wish to be the custodian at Casa Bianca. His paradise was disenchanted.

Clara stopped to gather some flowers growing beside the footpath. When she looked up, her brow was smooth, and her eyes untroubled. They spoke on other subjects till they reached the house, at the entrance of which they separated.

Neither of them referred to their early walk, nor to the grave under the mimosas and cypress trees. Donald knew all. A life's story had been revealed by a glance and a few words.

After the early breakfast, George and Donald took a

long walk; during which the cause of the youth's sudden
resolution to cross the Atlantic was explained.

"It is full time, Geordie, yes, more than full time, you
were at home again," Donald said, while honest enthusiasm flushed his fair face and lighted up his blue eyes. "I
did not half like the way things were going on, the last
time I was down at Redcastle. Such chaffering and col-
loguing, and that man, my mother's cousin, the lawyer,
who never loved you or your father, at the head and tail
of it all. My mother and I had a bitter quarrel when she
came up to Edinbro'; and I told her a bit of my mind,
after she said that the estate would have to be sold to pay
the Laird's debts, most of which, I am afraid, were of her
own incurring."

"Surely they cannot mean to sell my inheritance—the
Castle of my ancestors!" said George angrily. "That cannot be done without the heir's sanction."

"I don't know," said Donald doubtfully. "There has
been a lot of money raised upon the property—more than
it is worth, my mother says. There was talk of an Act of
Session to enable your father to sell the estate, but I doubt
whether he is in a condition of mind to act upon it.

"I told my mother you should know what was passing,"
Donald continued, still more indignantly, "but she only
smiled, and said that I was quite at liberty to write what I
liked. She only feared that your father's affairs were in
such an entangled state that it would take wiser heads
than hers, or yours, or mine, to clear off the embarrass-

ments which were pressing upon him. He often grew very impatient when she tried to control the expenditure."

George could not restrain a bitter smile.

"If so, it is your mother's kith and kin who are eating us out of house and home, Donald. While my father was able to govern his family, as you well know, the person to whom you have alluded was not numbered among the guests invited to Redcastle."

"Trust me, Geordie, for reminding her of that," answered Donald; "and also for telling her I was afraid she had not been faithful to her trust in ruling over the household when its lawful head was unequal to the task. It was hard to have to say such things to my own mother, but I did not spare her. I am sure the others are egging her on and misleading her. When she was gone, I made up my mind to come and tell you as well as I could how matters stood; and I can only say again—if you ever hope to take your bonnie bride to Redcastle, you had better lose no time in looking after your own interests in Scotland."

George saw that the youth suspected more than filial duty allowed him to touch upon, and would not press him with further questions. He was much too honourable to endure any concealment, and therefore judged it right to impart to Madame and her son the reasons for Donald's journey; and that he might have to return with him to their native country, in order to secure a future home for Rozay.

Madame listened kindly, and yielded to his entreaties

rather to hasten than to retard the marriage, for which the preparations were now completed. But on one point she was firm: Rozay should not go to that remote, barbarous land till all was settled.

Madame confessed that she had a sort of terror with regard to those distant isles of the sea which belonged to Great Britain, and did not appear to be quite certain whether their inhabitants were civilized Christians, or Pagans. London was all very well; and parts of England where she had been staying with her husband, who often talked of returning there. But the mountains and moors, the lakes and morasses, north of the Solway Firth, inspired her with vague alarm which she could not shake off.

George argued with her in vain. All the Highlander's love for his country, for the beautiful hills and glens, heath-clad heights, and burns trickling through green valleys, could not dispel her prejudices.

As the Chevalier had given his consent, and all was ready, she would not prevent or retard the nuptials. George might accompany them to Lisbon, and from thence proceed to Scotland, but Rozay must be left under her guardian's care.

When matters were settled at Redcastle, Mackenzie might come and claim his wife; who, meanwhile, would remain safely and happily with her adopted parents and sister on the banks of the Tagus, as she had dwelt at Casa Bianca during the years of her girlhood.

To this decision George was forced reluctantly to submit. It was a consolation that Rozay was not to be torn from him before he had a legal right to claim her as his wife. Rozay timidly acquiesced, though she longed to go with him to the land of his birth.

But it was a struggle to part from her kind friends, especially from Clara, whose dark eyes flashed with joy which had not shone in them since Philip Lavigne's death, when she found that, for the present at all events, she and her sister-cousin were not to be separated.

When this was arranged, no further discussion was permitted, and they all joined in making his short stay amongst them pleasant to Donald. The beautiful scenery was explored as far as time permitted, and in the evenings they all assembled in the wide veranda to listen to soft music, and to see the boys and girls belonging to the compound dance in the moonlight. Donald was the merriest among them, and executed wonderful Scotch steps as he showed them his national reels and the genuine Highland fling.

Still better, though his first brief love-dreams had come to an end, did the youth love to linger with Clara—while George and Rozay, now privileged lovers, wandered on far ahead—by the side of the river, and to hear her sweet voice speak of her regret at quitting her early home.

Some faint hopes sprang up in his mind when she confessed that her dream in life was to share, at least for a time, the northern home of George and Rozay. The two girls had never been parted, and she could not realize a separate existence from one so fondly loved.

Now that her brother had returned she hoped that her parents, who seldom denied her anything in reason, would consent to spare her. She did not share Madame's prejudices. Scotland was for her no barbarous desert, but a land of lakes and mountains, set in the blue sea, which she longed to visit.

Morag had inspired her with the enthusiasm which she felt for the country of her birth. George had made them love the whole Highland race. She wanted to see the rosy Castle in which he was born, by Beauly Firth.

Donald could have listened for ever to those melting accents, have gazed untired for years on that animated face, those darkly kindling eyes, full of southern fire, subdued, but not quenched.

He was young - he was hopeful. Might it not be that in the years to come—when time had set the signet of manliness on his brow, adding dignity to his bearing—that this fair creature, beautiful beyond all other women in his eyes, might lay aside mournful retrospections, and live and love again in the fresh atmosphere which breathes among the hills of the North, in his ain bonnie land?

PART THE FIFTH.

"For thee the wild grape glistens
  On sunny knoll and tree,
And stoops the slim papayo
  With yellow fruit for thee.
For thee the duck, on glassy stream,
  The prairie-fowl, shall die;
My rifle for thy feast shall bring
  The wild swan from the sky;
The forest's leaping panther,
  Fierce, beautiful, and fleet,
Shall yield his spotted hide to be
  A carpet for thy feet.

"Or wouldst thou gaze at tokens
  Of ages long ago—
Our old oaks stream with mosses
  And sprout with mistletoe;
And mighty vines, like serpents, climb
  The giant sycamore;
And trunks o'erthrown for centuries
  Cumber the forest floor;
And in the great savannah,
  The solitary mound,
Built by the elder world, o'erlooks
  The loneliness around.

"Come, thou hast not forgotten
  Thy pledge and promise quite,
With many blushes murmured,
  Beneath the evening light.
Come, the young violets crowd my door,

Thy earliest look to win,
And at my silent window-sill
The jessamine peeps in;
All day the red-bird warbles
Upon the mulberry near,
And the night sparrow trills his song,
All night, with none to hear."

THE HUNTER'S SERENADE.

CHAPTER XX.

"I know, for thou hast told me,
    Thy maiden love of flowers;
Ah, those that deck thy gardens
    Are pale compared to ours.
When our wide woods and mighty lawns
    Bloom to the April skies,
The earth has no more gorgeous sight
    To show to human eyes.
In meadows red with blossoms,
    All summer long, the bee
Murmurs and loads his yellow thigh
    For thee, my love, and me."

WILLIAM CULLEN BRYANT.

Willingly would George have carried his young bride to such a home as the American hunter invites his love to share,

"Where old woods overshadow the green savannah's side,"

or have taken her to the settler's allotment in New Brunswick, close to Morag and Fraser's land, which perhaps some day might be their destined home.

But his prospects as the heir of Redcastle, uncertain as they might be, were too fair to be relinquished without a struggle. His heart, - or at least as much of it as was still his own—was in the Highlands. That ardent love of the mountaineer for his native hills inspired him with fortitude to leave for a time the woman he loved so fondly, in the hope of placing himself in a position which might seem to her guardian more worthy of her claims.

It is not necessary to dwell on the short stay in the beautiful city on broad Savannah's banks which preceded the marriage, nor on the very simple ceremony, performed with all necessary formalities, according to the custom of our Church in that country, as well as of that to which Rozay and her family belonged, but without any pomp or parade.

All that remains of it is the certificate setting forth briefly that George Mackenzie and Rozay Angelica Perpetua Morais, by license from His Excellency the Governor, were united in holy matrimony by the minister of the English Church at Savannah, in Georgia, on the 22nd of March, 1781.

Donald performed the task of best man, we may be sure, and Clara was the solitary bridesmaid. Her own feelings were sufficiently under control to prevent her saddening the joyful occasion; she was too true a friend and sister to yield to them. The Scottish youth thought that she looked more like an angel than ever, as she stood beside Rozay in her simple white dress, without jewel or ornament of any description, excepting a snowy lily which fastened back the nun-like veil that shrouded her dark hair.

There were hours of wandering in the green woods fringing the banks of the noble river; and then a solemn parting, which all felt to be sad, from the country where so many happy years had been spent. Although peace had not yet been proclaimed, owing to the dissensions in the English Parliament, then even more bitter than now, the war was virtually at an end—the great Colony was free.

George experience no difficulty in obtaining leave of absence to visit his native country on urgent private business. As he had been previously settled, he and Rozay accompanied Madame and her son and daughter to Lisbon, where Don Diego fervently gave his blessing to the young couple and wished George good speed on his further journey.

He cordially approved of Madame's decision, and received Rozay again gladly, giving her a home like his own daughter in the beautiful palace which had suffered so severely from the great earthquake; but had now been entirely restored and of late much embellished, in preparation for the return of its mistress.

Don Diego was in great favour at Court, and much occupied in carrying out some of the benevolent and patriotic measures inaugurated by the great Minister now languishing in exile at a distance from the capital which he had well-nigh rebuilt.

But since the death of the great and wise monarch, who had supported Pombal even more constantly than Henry the Fourth upheld Sully, darkness had fallen upon the land.

An absolute monarchy weakly administered is the greatest burden a nation can groan under. The sun had sunk below the horizon, and numbers of twinkling luminaries strove in vain to supply the place of the wisely advised King who knew how to reward, protect, and support his faithful counsellor.

For many years of his later life Pombal consecrated the day of his own birth by the most solemn and devotional exercises. He was now past his eightieth birthday, and he awaited with Christian fortitude and resignation the approaching hour of death. The links of family love, always held precious by him, were drawn yet closer by the illustrious statesman, and the tender attentions of his children, especially his eldest son, soothed his declining years.

The motto placed beneath the picture of Pombal and his brothers at the Castle of Oeyras, "Concordia Fratrem," exemplifies their union. These brothers died before him, unmarried, leaving to him their united fortunes.

Pombal's eldest son accompanied Don John the Sixth in his emigration to Brazil, and died there, childless, in the year 1812.

It was a saying of Pombal's, that he feared but two things—children and fools.

It is perhaps not generally known that Pombal introduced the use of forks in Portugal, bringing them with him from England, on his return from the Court of St.

James, in 1745.

Even the power and malice of the Marquis de Pombal's numerous enemies and detractors could not efface from the minds of his fellow-countrymen the memory of the man on whose grave was inscribed the epitaph afterwards obliterated by order of the Government.

Let us bid farewell to the great statesman who passed away from earth with quiet dignity, regretted by all who knew him intimately, by the poor, and by all lovers of justice and humanity—in the words of that probably forgotten memorial:

EPITAPH TO SEBASTIAN JOSEPH DE CARVALHO
E MELLO, ETC., ETC.

After having rebuilt Lisbon,
Reanimated Commerce,
Created Manufactures,
Restored Learning,
Established the Laws,
Restrained Vice,
Recompensed Virtue,
Punished Hypocrisy,
Repressed Fanaticism,
Made the Sovereign Authority respected:
Loaded with Glory,
Crowned with Laurels,
Oppressed with Calumny,
Lauded by all Foreign Nations,
Abused by his own;
Equal to Richelieu in the greatness of his
designs,
Like Sully in his life and lot,
Great in prosperity,
Lofty in adversity;

Leaving ample materials
For the wonder and praise of future ages,
As philosopher, hero and Christian,
He passed into Eternity,
In the eighty-third year of his age
And the twenty-seventh of his ministry,
The Fifth of May, 1782.
May the earth repose lightly upon him.

———

CHAPTER XXI.

"I stood on the shore while the sad twilight drew
    Its grey veil across the blue heaven;
And the deep-thoughted stars all looked holily
        through
    The vast brooding vault of the even;
And numbers of fancies came crowding on me
    As I gazed on the desolate sea.

"I thought of the long sunny days of my youth,
    When I dwelt by the murmuring billow;
Of the yellow-ribbed sands and the pebbles so
        smooth,
    Of the beck that crept down by the willow;
And dreams of my childhood were borne unto
        me
    In the dimple and dash of the sea.

"I thought of a ship sailing into the West,
    Of hearts on her dewy deck grieving,
Of the tear-burdened eyelid, the quivering breast,
    The sigh for the land they are leaving;
And the passionate farewell was wafted to me
    In the ripple and rush of the sea."

                                        W. Leighton.

All George Mackenzie's life passed in review before him when he stood, months afterwards, - for alternate storms and calms had delayed his return to Scotland,

and the wonders of the steam were then unknown—on the shore of the Beauly Firth, looking seaward.

He felt himself, once more, a happy, heedless boy, in his mother's lifetime, roaming through the Redcastle woods; or wandering by the water-side, following the burn, fishing-rod and tackle in hand and slung on his back, or launching his boat on the briny estuary. Sometimes lying lazily on the sand-heaps watching the sun go down among the gorgeous clouds in the west.

The passionate sorrow he had felt when he lost his mother, followed by wild rage in his boyish heart when that sweet household angel was unworthily replaced—the years of alternate neglect and tyranny which led to his cutting asunder all home ties and casting himself adrift, a waif and stray upon the desolate sea of life—all passed in succession before him.

He saw the outward-bound ship with its crowded decks and apparently hopeless confusion. Once more there rose up before him faces he had seen and never forgotten—girls and mothers clinging to the necks of beardless boys, whom they might never, perhaps, behold again. Sailors with tears flowing down their rough sunburnt cheeks for the lasses left behind them. Partings between wife and husband, child and parent!

All that had passed before him as he stood alone, envying those who had friends to bid them "God speed ye" on their way—little more than a boy, unmourned, departing from his native country, without a hand to press, or a voice to murmur through tears—"Farewell"!

George had not entered a house or asked a question since he and Donald set foot on the shore of Britain. They hurried on together, as quickly as their not over abundant means and the indifferent mode of travelling permitted, to the goal of their thoughts and hopes—the Mackenzie's country.

It had been a hard struggle to part with Rozay, his young, tender, beautiful wife. George felt as if his heart was breaking when Donald urged upon him to return to Scotland. Life was so sunny on the banks of the Tagus, in the fair Palace where they were such welcome guests, and where Rozay was now wafting passionate sighs, in her dreary solitude, across the sea to her lover-husband.

Nature had seemed adverse to him ever since they parted, for the prosperous voyage to Lisbon had been followed, after a brief interval of sunshine and happiness on land, by the wildest weather on the sea. George would not believe what Donald told him, that they had let the summer go by in idleness, and must pay for it now. It seemed but a day that he had passed among the orange and lemon groves of Portugal.

Be that as it may—it is useless to expect lovers to reckon faithfully weeks and months as they fly past—the stormy season had come on before they left the Lisbon Palace. The sailing-packet proved to be a very different vessel from the fine ship which had been appointed by the Queen to bring home the family of her favoured Minister. Storm after storm swept across their course, followed by baffling calms, provisions ran short, shipwreck was narrowly escaped when the winds rose again tumultuously. At last, after manifold dangers and delays, the crazy vessel came into port.

George felt afraid even to guess what might have happened. He pushed on across the country; now wearying Donald by his impatience, as much as he had provoked him by dilatoriness before starting. The poor youth was utterly exhausted when they reached their last resting-place, before entering their native county. George left him there to his much-needed repose, and hurried on alone.

Footsore and weary after his long tramp, for he had not been able to procure a horse, and would not await the return of the only vehicle the rude inn they had slept at last could boast of possessing, - George Mackenzie pursued his course; growing, as he went on, more familiar with the features of the country, and making his way as straight as a die, over moss and moor, to the home of his boyhood.

He did not enter the small hostelry on the banks of the Firth, where he had spent weary hours of sickness on his last visit to Scotland. Now he was resolved to see his father. No human power should keep him from hearing, if it must be so, from Muckle Colin's own lips, his sentence of banishment.

There was not much fear of recognition even in his own neighbourhood, unless he chose to reveal himself, for George was much altered in appearance. The Moustache which now covered his upper lip, had during the voyage, been allowed to grow bushy. It concealed the sweet smiling mouth of the boy who had been a favourite far and wide, as much as the foraging cap pulled low on his brow darkened its fairness.

His figure, taller and more slender, had a military air, widely differing from that of the shy, stalwart country youth. Many might have deemed him a foreigner; few would have dreamed that the grave officer, with abstracted looks pacing the yellow sands, was the light-hearted boy who had so often traversed them of yore on some errand of sport or mischief.

But there were not many persons about; the weather was gloomy, night coming on, when George after rowing himself across the estuary in a boat, which he had found moored under a willowy bank, and depositing a liberal fee for its use in the safest place he could select, sent it adrift, and entered his ancestral woods.

He had a fancy to see how the old place would look from the summer-house where he had spent uneasy nights after first leaving home, where his faithful allies, Donald and Morag, had visited him. George could not help thinking that he should be able to trace, even in the outline of those rosy walls and towers, some sign of a welcome home.

But no roseate hue overspread the ancient Highland Castle when, with deep emotion, the heir of the Mackenzies first caught sight of it through the trees. Dark and dull, with not one gleam of light, the towers and turreted battlement loomed above the almost leafless boughs.

George went down close to the water's edge where there was, as he well knew, an unimpeded prospect of his birthplace. Here he had stood with Morag watching the glancing light in the windows when the old house was full of gay company. And on this spot he had, after the kind brother and sister left him, remained in utter solitude, watching the red lightning flash above the grove and glitter on the high casements.

Even the storm would have seemed better to him than this dull weird silence. The roll of thunder, the electric flashes would have wakened him from the dull dread lethargy creeping over him, as he looked at the old castle—grey and dim—not a token of life within or outside its walls; rising up, grand and gloomy, against the clouded evening sky.

Now that he had lost his opportunity, George would have given worlds to question someone as to what had passed latterly in that silent house. A feeling that death was in the heavy air that hung above the woods, grew and gathered strength within him. For the first time he felt his own utter weariness. Mind and body were alike exhausted.

The breeze, which sprang up suddenly, instead of reviving, seemed to pierce through every fold of his raiment, cutting him to the heart like a knife. He retreated to the summer-house, and throwing himself on the rough bench which had served him for a couch, burst into tears which did not shame his manhood.

He felt himself once more a boy in the woods—exiled from home—abjured by his kindred—ignorant of what might have befallen the old man, who, in the days long past, had been a kind and loving father.

George started up, when, suddenly, the Castle bell pealed over the woods. It was the first token of life that had greeted him. The sound, dirge-like and solemn, told, however, no tale to his listening ears. All that it revealed was that someone there must be in the great house, still breathing and living.

The night had deepened as he walked back by the shore of the loch. The boat had not drifted far, and he succeeded in catching hold of the chain and bringing it back to the landing-stage. He dared not follow out his first intention of going boldly up to the Castle, and demanding admission. He felt that he must wait for the morning to give him fresh spirits, strength and courage.

CHAPTER XXII.

I thought of wild moments of ruin and wrath,
    Of mad billows tossing and seething;
Of a proud vessel swept from the tempest's
        dread path—
Of a low wind above her grave breathing;
And some of Death's secrets were whispered
        to me
    In the howling and rush of the sea.

I thought of the peace of a heavenly shore,
    Of a land where no broad sea can sever;
Of a glad light which sorrow can darken
        no more,
    Of a rest to the weary for ever.
And a chorus of angels seemed breathed
        unto me
    In the tremor and thrill of the sea.

The many storms he had encountered on his weary homeward passage across the ocean, after parting from his bride, seemed surging and boiling in Mackenzie's ears as he walked slowly up from the shore of the estuary to the inn, where he had been so kindly treated and welcomed on his last visit to the Highlands.

He longed to question the friendly old servants respecting the changes which might have occurred at Redcastle—

and yet an over-powering dread seemed to tie his tongue. He walked still more slowly as he drew near the house and sometimes stopped, lost in thought.

More than once when he was on the sea, with the superstition of a Highlander of one of those ancient races whose embers are supposed to see more than ordinary sons of earth, Mackenzie had seen, or imagined, omens of misfortune in the sights and sounds upon the stormy face of the deep.

One night, in particular, after the ship had been in dire peril, while the sea still heaved after the tempest which had wrecked a vessel, dimly distinguished in the mist, which they were unable to aid, George had watched the wild glancing lights on the tops of the billows, curling round the track of the ship, and resembling the torches borne over his native hills at a Highland funeral. He remembered well seeing such a procession in his boyhood, when his mother was borne to the grave, to be buried among her husband's kindred.

A voice had seemed to come to him, then, across the troubled waters of the Bay of Biscay, first murmuring in the shrouds, then growing louder and more threatening. Could it have been telling him that, at that very hour of solemn midnight, in as wild a storm as had just ceased to rage over the sea, relays of his old retainers had borne the bowed form, once so stalwart and stately, of his father, the last Laird of Redcastle, to his grave?

Mackenzie tried in vain to banish the forebodings of

evil which were gathering round him, and which the dull damp night-air and solitude fostered. He moved on more quickly when he saw the lights of the Highland inn shining out across the road, but here, again, disappointment awaited him.

Though the hour was late, the landlord and his wife were stirring, and came to the door to greet the weary traveller. There was no fear, or hope, of recognition; both were complete strangers, and by their speech and manner English-born. They were very civil, and busied themselves with attending to the wants of their guest, apologizing for some deficiencies by the excuse that they had but lately come to the place, and were strange to the ways of north-country folk.

Mackenzie was too weary to question them. He did not make himself known, but retired at once to a room which was kept ready for any belated wanderer. He was too sick at heart to desire food.

The room was very quiet. Lulled by the only sound which reached his ears, that of the waves on the beach, and by the well-remembered scent of peat on which the snowy linen had been dried, Mackenzie fell asleep soon after laying his head upon the pillow. He did not dream of his early home wrapped in the evening shadows, or of his young bride in the Lisbon palace. Thought was too tired to take further flights.

He rose very early, but not before there was light in the room, and, dressing himself hastily, went out before the other inmates of the house were stirring. The fastenings were familiar to him, and few precautions were necessary in that quiet place. It was his custom, he told the landlord, to rise betimes and take a walk before breakfast. If a young man called to inquire about him, a fellow-traveller who had broken down at the last stage of their long journey, he might either wait for him, or follow him to the summer-house in the Redcastle woods on the opposite shore of the loch.

He took possession of the boat again, and rowed himself over to the landing-place, making the boat fast at the little pier, as he meant to return by the same way. Other boats were kept at the ferry; and, if Donald came to the waterside, there would be people stirring by that time at the cottage.

Mackenzie had a great longing to be alone in the woods for a while in the early morning, before revealing himself to any of his own people and making further inquiries. He dreaded the results unspeakably; and fancied he could bear better to hear from his adopted brother's lips than from any others', whatever there might be to tell.

The first sunbeam that struck the walls of the old sandstone castle brought out its rosy hue. George breathed more freely, but the next moment he started, and walked down to the water's edge. There was a flag flying from the highest tower, which he did not recognise. It was not that of his house.

He looked again and again, but his eyes seemed strangely

dim, and the wind made the folds flap so that he could distinguish neither colours nor device plainly. But he was sure it was not the flag which had floated on the breeze above the serried ranks of his kindred in many a foray. He threw himself down on the bank, and watched it waving above the battlements in speechless wonder.

George did not know how long he had watched and waited before a step sounded on the gravel-path, and Donald came up and joined him. His grave face prepared his adopted brother for evil tidings, but not for the full account of his budget. In a few moments Mackenzie had learnt that his father was dead, and had been dead many months, and that strangers were dwelling at Redcastle.

"Cheer up, dear old fellow," Donald said, tenderly clasping his hand—"each cloud has its silver lining—when things come to the worst they must mend; and, truly, you and I are about at the end of our tether. You at all events have nothing to blush for; but I am afraid that I and mine have wrought fearful ill to your ancient house, since my mother became your father's wife."

"Let that rest," said George, gravely, rousing himself from his bitter grief.

"You and Morag are in no way responsible for what has come and gone. In my darkest hour you both stood by me. I shall never forget who brought me food and consolation when I was hiding in these dark woodlands. Now tell me all that you know. I am a man again and can bear it."

"It is but little I can tell you," said Donald; "I do not half understand it myself. All I know is that the estate—'drowned in debt,' as my informant told me - after a certain proclamation and a lapse of a period sufficient, in the eyes of the law, for the next heir to protest against it, - was sold to the highest bidder—and that he is dwelling at Redcastle now."

George looked again at the towers rising above the woods.

"And so farewell to all my greatness," he said with a sigh. The wind had blown the flag right round the flagstaff. No device was visible, and the sun hidden behind clouds ceased to bring out the rosy colour of the stone.

"Donald let us go back to the Inn. We are nothing but trespassers here."

The two young men walked down together, without speaking another word, to the water's edge. When they were in the boat rowing across the estuary, which, as if to mock the hopes of the young heir, was again bright with sunshine, Donald said:

"My only comfort is that I believe my mother had been as much cheated as yourself. I believe that he and his confraternity have feathered their own nests and left her out in the cold. She is living quietly, the Landlord at the Inn tells me, in Edinburgh—and, Geordie, she *was kind* to the old man, your father, to the last. On that point we are all agreed."

George bowed his head over the oar in silence. He was thinking less of his lost inheritance than of having missed receiving his father's blessing and forgiveness.

CHAPTER XXIII.

When sorrow sleepeth, wake it not,
    But let it slumber on;
If grief is for a while forgot,
    Its power that while is gone.

The mind may from the pause gain strength
    To grapple with its foe,
And thence may rise to prove at length
    Victorious over woe.

Then watch thy thoughts, thy words restrain,
    Each heart its burden knows,
One little word, all light and vain,
    May break that heart's repose.

Donald respected George's deep grief; and, after his fervent ejaculation, there was silence till they reached the shore, where they found a small group of people collected, news having gone through the place that the foreign officer, as he had been called, was no other than the youth they remembered well as once—The Master of Redcastle.

There were some cordial greetings, but they were mostly silent ones - grasps of the hand—tears flowing down manly, sunburnt faces—offers of hospitality from honest though humble friends—a message from the Castle not far distant, where Fraser's kindred would gladly have welcomed his friend—but George declined them all. His heart was too sore for sympathy.

He went quietly back to the Inn, and shut himself up in his own room, till he had schooled himself to face his altered fortunes. Late in the day, having made inquiries respecting the former managers of the Inn, old family servants of the Mackenzies, and belonging to the place, George learnt they were carrying on the same business not far away. He sent on his own and Donald's small amount of luggage, which the latter had brought with him, to their next resting-place.

Mackenzie had no wish to linger within the sight of Redcastle, and he longed to hear more of his father's last hours of life, and of the circumstances attending his death. Gossip was rife among the small community living near his birthplace; but he closed his ears against hearing idle talk which might stir up wrath, and induce him to utter words which he might hereafter wish had been unsaid.

The current of the Beauly River was running strong as George and Donald walked beside it, sadly enough in the evening, toward Kessoch Ferry. As they looked back from the boat in mid-passage, bright beams were descending, which separated the wooded hills and fell across the Beauly and Moray Firths, lighting up in solemn farewell the crimsoned walls of the sandstone castle, and glittering in its many windows.

Before they landed darkness had fallen, and the lamps of the quaint old Capital of the North-western Highlands soon began to sparkle at intervals through the trees as they drove rapidly, in a hired carriage, along the banks of the Ness. The high mountain ranges stood out against the pale grey wintry sky, but the deep valleys were full of gloom.

> "And up the hills, on either side, a wood
> Of blackening pines, aye waving to and fro,
> Sent forth a sleepy horror through the blood."

A very warm welcome awaited Mackenzie at the Inn kept by the former servants of his family. Their familiar, home-like faces cheered the desolate travellers; and, although Donald was not exactly the rose, he came in its company and shared it honours.

No one could be better qualified to speak of the old Laird's last moments than the host of The Mackenzie Arms, as the new Inn was called; for he had assisted in waiting upon him more than once when especial care and discretion were required; leaving his wife to manage the business, when he was summoned to the Castle.

"Many a time at the last, did the poor old master cry out for his only and only son," the faithful servant said, with emotion. "Madame was sorry enough that she had come between, and parted, father and child! At one time the Laird was under a delusion, believing that some imposter bearing your name had come to the Castle; but his mind cleared towards the end and his thoughts went back to the past—to the dear lady, your mother, we all loved so well, and to his only child."

The Highlander's face flushed indignantly as he went on speaking, and his own changed from sorrow to anger.

"Never believe, master, that he was in his right senses when he bade the servants leave you outside the door! It's not for me to say the cause, but he was sorely misguided. The mistress would have given more than she had gotten off the estate to have been able to undo the wrong she did in making the old house too hot to hold you. She's greatly changed, and living quite in a small way they say in Edinbro', not a bit of the grand lady now."

George heard with satisfaction that his father's heart had softened towards him before he died, and that his step-mother had become less bitter. The old family servants confirmed Donald's report of her devoted attention to her husband during his illness. Out of respect for his father's memory, Mackenzie determined that he would visit and take leave of her before quitting, probably for ever, his native land.

On the following morning George called upon the Factor, and made more particular investigation into the forced sale of the estate. We are not able to enter into the details of a Scotch suit, nor is it necessary to say more than that all legal formalities had been observed. There was no link into which light could penetrate in that dark transaction, no ground on which an objection could be raised.

The estate, heavily encumbered, had been sold by act of Session, to the highest bidder, and was his by right of law. The absence of the heir, after due notice had been given to afford time for a protest on his part against the sale, was held to justify the proceedings instituted.

In after years, when the lands and Castle were again in the market, an offer of them was made to the husband of George Mackenzie's eldest daughter, our own father; an English gentleman residing in the Midland Counties on his own property, but not in sufficiently affluent circumstances to become the purchaser of so valuable an estate.

Ultimately Redcastle was bought by the father of the present owner. The grand-daughters of George Mackenzie and Rozay Morais were courteously entertained there, some years ago, under the roof of the old Castle, built by William the Lyon, and intended by him for a royal habitation.

The ancient Tower, overlooking the Estuary, and rising above the beautiful terraced gardens and groves, still grows red in the sunset and grey in the dusk. The waves of the Beauly loch lap the pebbles on the spot where Morag and Donald brought food by stealth to the boy who was then the undoubted heir of Redcastle.

CHAPTER XXIV.

Only a dog! Yes, only,
   Yet these are bitter tears,
Weary and homesick and lonely,
   I turn to the coming years.

A form that was once familiar,
   A heart I could always trust,
A friend who always loved me,
   Lies moldering here to dust.

Faithful and loving and tender,
   Gentle and generous and brave,
My pet, my playmate, my darling,
   And this is his lonely grave.

"Yes, the old Colley was always true to his trust," said the faithful clansman, Evan Mackenzie, the Landlord of the Inn, as he and George stood together in a distant part of the policies of Redcastle, looking down upon a green mound under a fir tree.

"When you left home you told him to take care of the old Master, and he did it to the best of his ability. They were seldom parted."

George remembered that Fraser had seen the Laird and his dog together, when he caught sight of his friend's father in the plantations.

"After all," he said mournfully, "the dog was truer to the old Master than his own son; I wish that I had stayed by him to the last."

"That could scarcely be," said Evan. "Men can ill bear the cuts and curbings which a dog will take from the hand that feeds him. Your father, however, was always kind to the dumb creatures—they never chafed his temper or disputed his will. The colley crept after him when his footsteps were slow and halting just as it had sprung before him, when his foot was light in the heather. I found him lying dead just here, where he often sat with his Master, two days after the funeral, and I buried him myself, in this quiet spot. You see no one has ventured to disturb him."

"I thank you, Evan, for this and many another pious care," said George, laying his hand kindly on the trusted retainer's shoulder, as they turned away together.

"You did your utmost to supply my father's needs and the loss of his absent son. Now I am come back, homeless and powerless, and can do little to repay you. All that is pleasant of the memories of Redcastle rest with you and your good wife, who was like a mother to me in my forlorn childhood. You must order for me a stone to be put up in memory of my old favourite, who lies yonder under the fir tree, and ask the new comers to respect the spot."

"Yes, I'll do that, though I bear them no love," said Evan. "Is it not strange to think that utter strangers should hold their court in the old house, and that you and I, Mackenzies born, should have no right to enter? Not that I want ever to cross that threshold again, where we were once at peace and trusted; and you have little cause to love the place whence you have been long banished."

George looked round, sorrowfully, after the faithful servant of his family had left him.

"And yet I do love every stone of the old house in which I was born, every tree in these woods, even the pebbles on the loch shore," he said to Donald, who had come from the Inn to meet him and had heard the Landlord's last words. "Hark how the waves come lapping in over them. It is a sound I loved to lie and listen to in boyhood. Let us go down to the water's edge."

They went down together and threw themselves side by side on the beach, while the wind swayed the tree-tops with a melancholy cadence, and the waves rippled over the sand, among the pebbles.

"Mind what I say, George. Mark my words," said the youth, suddenly raising himself on his elbow. "If ever I am a rich man, and I do not intend to be an idle one, I shall make up to you for the grievous wrong my mother has done to you. Morag's portion—my legal training—all that we have, or shall have, has come from the estate which melted away in hers and your poor father's fingers. I am the Steward for the debt of your lost inheritance."

"Heed it not , my boy," said George cordially, grasping

his extended hand. "As I told your mother, yesterday, when I saw her in Edinburgh, - all that is past—is past - and if it is not quite forgotten—forgiven. I shall never make further inquiries into it. The estate of my fathers has passed away to strangers. Our lands, our money, are neither hers, nor yours, nor mine. There can be no stewardship when the property has altogether been lost. I have my own mother's small fortune which was luckily settled upon me. With this and the handsome portion given at our marriage to my wife by her kind Guardian-Uncle, we shall be more than content—we shall be gloriously happy— though we may not live in the old Highland Castle. These are sad moments, but they are, like all earth's day-dreams, passing away."

He rose as he spoke, inaction being painful to him, and linking his arm in Donald's, they walked to the ferry together. Not one backward glance did Mackenzie give, as he crossed the water and returned to the ancient city, to the bonnie lands which he was no longer able to regard as his inheritance.

We shall strictly follow our young hero's example, and if we cannot always extenuate, try to set down nought in malice. All that concerns our partly veracious chronicle is that, through grievous mismanagement, the estate passed away from the old family into the hands of strangers, as many another has done before it, and, probably, will do hereafter.

For several years the old Laird had been incompetent for the management of his affairs, and the persons about him had taken advantage of his feebleness of mind. Now that he was gone to his grave filial respect forbade the raising a cloud of suspicion, and George refused to enter into what his friendly lawyer advised him might prove a useless, and must be a painful investigation.

"Muckle Colin" slept with his ancestors! "Peace be to his ashes:" the good son whispered, after kneeling by that Highland sepulchre, where both his parents had been laid with all customary honours, and giving directions that it should be carefully kept in order.

How passing strange it is that in a country where so much value is attached to a family burial-ground, so many ancient graveyards shock a stranger by their aspect of utter desolation. Rank weeds and nettles hide the inscriptions and forbid approach to the tombstones on which many noble historic names are inscribed in country burial-grounds of Scotland.

There were two places of sepulture connected with our narrative which were not thus left neglected. Donald kept sacred the promise made, at parting, to his adopted brother, before he crossed the Channel, and constantly visited both. Evan Mackenzie, too, often stood by the graves of his old master, and that other, humbler, faithful follower.

Over the last earthly resting-place of the kindly, choleric, weak-minded giant, a handsome monument was raised, befitting his station, while a modest stone under the Scotch fir-tree recorded the virtue and fidelity of the old dog, whose loving heart broke after he followed the Laird for the last time to his grave among the Mackenzies of Redcastle.

SUNSHINE AFTER SHADOW.

As I look from the Isle o'er its billows of green,
To the billows of foam-crested blue,
Yon bark that afar in the distance is seen,
Half-dreaming my eyes will pursue:
Now dark in the shadow, she scatters the spray
As the chaff in the stroke of the flail,
Now white as the seagull she flies on her way,
The sun glancing bright on her sail.

Yet her pilot is thinking of dangers to shun -
Of breakers that whiten and roar—
How little he cares if in shadow or sun
They see him that gaze from the shore!
He looks to the beacon that looms from the surf,
To the rock that is under her lee,
As he drifts on the blast, like a wind-driven leaf,
O'er the gulfs of the desolate sea.

CHAPTER XXV.

"Oh for one hour of youthful joy!
  Give back my twentieth spring!
  I'd rather laugh a bright-haired boy,
  Than reign a gray-beard king.

"One moment let my life blood stream
  From boyhood's fount of flame,
  Give me one giddy, reeling dream
  Of life and love and fame.

     *   *   *   *

"Ah, truest soul of womankind,
  Without thee, what were life?
  One bliss I cannot leave behind,
  I'll take . . . my . . . precious wife.

"The Angel took a sapphire pen.
  And wrote in rainbow dew, -
  The man would be a boy again,
  And be a husband too!"

OLIVER WENDELL HOLMES.

Lisbon and beautiful Cintra were in festa when George Mackenzie, after long delays and a tedious sea voyage, returned to claim his wife. Early Spring in its freshness hung above the vineyards and olive groves; the leaves just shaking out their white linings, the outside green not wearing the dark dull hue of mid-summer, but sprouting forth gaily.

Royal festivities were going forward, and the Chevalier stood high in courtly favour; but, on the horizon, his far-seeing eyes already discerned the small cloud, not larger than a man's hand, which made him, some years afterwards, seek and obtain an official employment in the diplomatic service of his country, and exchange official life at Court for a home, unshadowed by bigotry, in England.

Though he had felt bitterly the destruction of all the dreams of his youth, and the banishment from his Highland home, George Mackenzie felt himself repaid for all he had lost when he clasped his young wife to his heart, and felt that death alone could part them.

War being now at an end, and peace proclaimed between England and her great revolted colony, he felt himself at liberty to retire honourably from active service. He had never recovered from the effect of the passage of the ball, though spent, across his chest, and life was very precious to him now.

It was hoped that care and a warmer climate than Scotland might restore him to health. The keen breezes of the Highlands, his hurried journeys, and the painful excitement of the last winter and autumn, had tried him greatly.

Though not rich, the young husband and wife were independent, and surrounded by kind friends. A tiny villa at Cintra, full of tokens of affection, received them when they were weary of the gaieties of the Capital; where a suite of apartments in the Chevalier's Palace was always reserved for their occupation.

Rozay's kind guardians were not, in their inmost hearts, grieved that the Highland Paradise had not opened its gates to receive her. She was once more a child of their house, sharing with Clara their love and protection, and George was as dear to them as a son of their own.

We shall adhere to the old-fashioned custom in fiction of leaving our hero and heroine during the early days of matrimony, before even the lightest clouds have obscured its sunshine. No doubt, like other mortals, Rozay Morais and George Mackenzie had darker days in store for them, but one thing we can vouch for, so long as they were allowed to remain together their love was undiminished.

Neither can we carry our readers across the Atlantic again to visit the far-off home we can picture to ourselves of Morag and Fraser, - the certificate of their marriage has not come down to us together with the faded lines testifying that George and Rozay were made one—but we can affirm positively that our grandfather's best loved friend and comrade in arms bore the name of Fraser, and that they were faithful to each other till death.

If Donald did not carry out his intentions of leaving to the children of his adopted brother the fortune of which, perhaps, the first nest-egg was laid in the bonnie woods of Redcastle, it was only because, after long years of celibacy, he took to himself a young wife, and had bairns enough of his own to inherit it.

Clara withstood all his pleadings and never married, nor were she and her sister-cousin ever separated. Like twin roses on one stalk, they lived together loving and beloved.

But it is not within our province to go farther. Let us leave them—this happy family group—just as they were when reunited by George's return from his bootless errand to his native country; with warm clear southern skies arching over the vine-wreathed front of the Quinta, amid the orange and lemon groves of Cintra.

POSTSCRIPT.

"And parted thus they rest, who played
  Beneath the same green tree;
Whose voices mingled as they prayed
  Around one parent knee,"

FELICIA HEMANS.

Widely apart are the resting-places of those who are already gone before us! The Graves of a Household, as the sweet poetess of our day once sang, are often "severed far and wide," "By mount and stream, and sea,"— though in infancy –

"The same fond mother bent at night
  O'er each fair sleeping brow;
She had each folded flower in sight,—
  Where are those dreamers now?"

I wonder whether I should love, as well as I once did, the flowery hedgerows and cowslip-covered meadows, where we used to roam freely in our childhood?

How well I remember those quiet rural haunts, the lanes which led nowhere, or only up to a high wall, and went by the name of Baulks, where bloomed sweet-scented violets, nestling among their dark leaves; not the nurslings from Naples, which have to be coaxed prematurely into flower; but the hardy, free, wild, white and purple darlings, that braved the winds of March, and grew yet more fragrant under April showers and sunshine.

Not long ago I spent a month in mid-summer at an old Hall in the midland counties, not far distant from my birthplace. The spire which rose heavenward above the old church close to the mansion, was a landmark of peculiar grace and beauty for all the country round.

Often, in our more sedate walks, when we were under the charge of our nurses or governess, I remember that we were taken to the top of a fir-crowned hill, about a mile from our house, to look at that lofty needle of grey stone, and many other church-towers and steeples, visible from that eminence in the flat country below, which belong to scattered villages half hidden among trees.

Afterward, in my girlhood, I had passed many happy weeks in a cottage on the outskirts of that pleasant village, where I first drew breath.

The dwelling where our dear friend lived and died, though close to the country road, was almost concealed from the passers along it by a row of elm trees, carefully kept clipped, after the fashion of her day.

This lady, the kind friend of my youth, whose place had once been among great and learned folk, now lived in tranquil retirement; but she had many a tale to tell of Lords and Ladies, Halls and Cities, to which I loved to listen. Half a dozen old servants, who, after serving faithfully different members of her family, had found rest and a home beneath her roof, waited respectfully upon her.

Often, during my stay at the Hall, when sounds of merriment, the noise of the cricket and tennis practice, mingling with the voices of children at play, came from the lawns and fields on the other side of the mansion, I would get out of the way of the balls, and almost beyond earshot of the cheering and laughter, and walk under the flowering limes of the churchyard below the beautiful spire; or go down to the ancient river, for it was the source and mother of a much wider, more famous stream, which Keats called "silver-footed."

The Old Trent, as it is named, winds somewhat sluggishly under the boughs of knotted alder-bushes and willows; sleeping in sunshine, which makes the yellow water-lilies on its tranquil bosom gleam like gold.

From the churchyard, with its many graves, - some quite humble and lowly, some mere grassy mounds, others adorned with lofty monuments, or more suitably, with simple crosses and head-stones decked with oft-renewed wreaths, - the ground fell steeply to the bed of the river.

Further down, the stream is crossed by a low bridge. I could lean over the parapet and watch the water flowing; flowing—flowing—as it had been flowing long before I was born and will probably flow on years after I, and all who once dwelt with me, or loved to gather together on the old house in the next county, repose under the green turf of other graveyards.

How would it have fared with us if we had remained in the home of our childhood, and been gathered to our rest near our father, who was buried under the shadow of the old trees which hang over the churchyard we crossed Sunday after Sunday? It was two miles away from our house, which stood at the entrance of another village; and there was great formality observed between the coachmen who drove the carriages of three or four neighbouring families.

It was not easy to restrain the paces of some of the more spirited steeds drawing lighter and more modern vehicles; but precedence was always yielded to a portly dame and her spouse, whose heavy coach, sleek carriage horses, and stout coachman and footman, matched each other exactly. Next came the dear good spinster, who dwelt in the bow-windowed cottage behind the clipped elms, - and we followed in their wake.

Well, it is of no use to surmise what we might have been, or done, if we had remained under the old roof-tree! It was not our wills to leave it; for we loved the village, the green lanes, commons and copses, and large, more distant woods. Most especially we loved the large garden at the back of the house where we played in childhood, and dreamed our dreams in early girlhood; dreams never destined to be fulfilled, but, perhaps, not sweeter, not brighter, than some that in the course of years have come to pass.

Of those fulfillments of what were then unconscious visions, but which must have had their birth in the library collected by our father, or by the sunk fence at the bottom of the lawn, or have been whispered in at our nursery windows by the wind moaning among the upper boughs of the great Scotch firs opposite, the best and brightest have been the accomplishment of some purposes which grew with our growth and strengthened with our strength, the power to write and paint, with pen and pencil (imperfectly, it may be, but truthfully), loved forms and features, the dreams of great masters, and the glorious beauty of earth, sea, and sky—the forest ranges, and the cloud-capped mountains.

> "Love had he found in huts where poor men lie,
>   His daily teachers had been wood and rills,
> The silence that is in the starry sky,
>   The sleep that is among the lonely hills."

To catch the humour of the moment, to soothe the mourner, and draw thought away from ills past remedy by some fresh tale of hardihood and adventure, these powers had been granted to us; and the gifts which have given pleasure to ourselves, and to many others, have not, we trust, been abused.

Of the two survivors of the group which once gathered at Christmas in the old home in the Shires, or under the trees in the garden on summer evenings, no record will remain save in the pictures and stories painted and written during their subsequent wanderings.

In the story now given to the public a curious family history is recorded, which must otherwise perish with them, and they have added to it some poems in which the interest centres in the family, and principally relates to their scattered graves.

One of the poems, "After Four Years' Separation," was written by the great-grand-daughter of the George Mackenzie, who was the last of that name who dwelt in the red sandstone castle beside the Beauly Water. Her own grave, which is described in the lines headed "Forget me Not," is among the Irish mountains; between the Galtee and Slieve-a-Rea chain of hills, one always blue and bright, the other dark and sombre, like the alternations of human life.

Another grave is under the Malvern Hills, as told in "The Vale of York," and "The Sister's Grave." In these poems there are illusions to the last earthly resting-places of our father, mother, and brothers, in the tranquil Midlands—near the south-western coast and downs of Dorset—and the silver sands of Guernsey.

AFTER FOUR YEARS' SEPARATION.

How little we thought when last together,
    Of the changes four years have made!
Of the links of love Death alone could sever;
    Of the scattered graves where our treasures
            are laid.

The little child was the first to go,
    As if to brighten the road:
We laid him to rest in his cradle low,
    With sweet flowers above his head.

We knew that for him, our precious one,
    God's angel had come in love,
And though, for awhile, our sunshine was gone,
    That our first-born would meet us above.

For the aged dear one the summons came,
    And she peacefully sank to her rest; -
A hallowed calm seems to hang round her name,
    Like the evening light in the west.

The path grew rough, and dark was the sky
    When the next of our band was called;
But to him Death came with one gentle sigh,
    And set free a spirit enthralled.

His lonely grave in a distant part
    Is tended by those who loved *him*,
And a sunny spot in many a heart
    Marks the friendship no time can dim.

In a shadowed nook, 'neath the grand old hills,
   We have opened a grave once more,
And a sole released from its mortal ills,
   Has reached the eternal shore.

But now when we mourn our dear ones flown,
   And our hearts grow sad and sore,
Let a thought of the blessings still left as our own,
   Send us upward and onward, once more.

E.C.F.

FORGET ME NOT!

Lay me where I may see my home,
  My children at their play,
Where those I love may often come
  And kneel, and weep, and pray.
With the grand mountains full in sight
  That gird my adopted land,
Dark Slieve-a-Rea—Galtees bright—
  Rising on either hand.

What matters if few flow'rets bloom
  On the rough broken ground;
That the mountain winds above my tomb
  Wail wildly, fiercely, round;
That the scathed trees are bent, and sway
  Beneath the tempest's power,
While storm-clouds dark, and cold, and grey,
  Above my lone grave lour?

See, there are rays of purest gold,
  Swift points of sun and shade,
Upon the Galtees' forehead bold
  By God's own finger laid.
Soft are the hues of distant heights,
  Green are those pastures fair,
Richer than even the mellowest lights
  Our English landscapes wear.

I'd rather feel the wild winds blow
  And see the mists sweep down,
Hiding yon mountain's lofty brow,
  Or circling round its crown,

Than watch the tranquil sunset's glow
    On many a sheltered home,
Or see the flowery garlands grow
    Round many a guarded tomb.

By choice this storm-swept rest is mine,
    Beneath yon ruined Tower,
Where moon and sun alternate shine,
    Ruling the appointed hour;
Where through the rent boughs overhead
    Swift showers and sunbeams pass,
And o'er the low homes of the dead
    Waves long, untrodden grass.

For love will brighten up the place,
    And make it smile once more,
Where the forefathers of our race
    Neglected lay of yore.
Each cumbering stone shall be removed,
    The turf shall slightly swell
O'er her who was so fondly loved,
    And loved in turn so well.

I'd rather be the first to tread
    In some fair earthly hall,
The first to love—the first to wed –
    And, ah!—the first to fall;
That mine should be the first green mound
    Reared in this lonely spot,
With blooming roses twined around:
    And oh!—Forget me not!

                        R. M. K.

THE VALE OF YORK.

Over the rich, low, level lands,
    Hung storm-clouds like a pall;
Dark and deep were those lurid bands—
    I knew that the bolt must fall.
Dim spires, and farms, and winding streams,
    Lay wrapt in mist, half seen,
With lowing kine and pausing teams
    Amid the pastures green.

At last, with a stunning, awful crash,
    The lowering skies are riven;
One loud sharp peal—one clear white flash –
    Straight down to earth from heaven.
No radiant colours flushed the sky,
    No sheet of flame spread round,
But a line of fire dropped from on high,
    Into the depths profound.

No zigzag lines of dazzling light
    Were written on the cloud,
But pale white folds of waving white
    Wound o'er it like a shroud.
Deep in my heart I heard a voice,
    With the thunder-music blent, -
Through the rushing rain-drops' arrowy noise,
    To me was a message sent.

Did it come from our father's quiet grave,
    Under the yew-tree's shade,
Where green boughs o'er the smooth turf wave,
    And meadow-blossoms fade?
Or from that peaceful, sacred bourne
    Where full of years and grace,
Our mother's hallowed form was borne
    To its last resting-place?

Was it sent from a lone grave far away,
    On a rock-besprinkled shore,
Where, tired and worn with earth's long day,
    Our brother rests once more?
Where tiny feet have often trod,
    And children's loving hands
Have laid wild flowers upon the sod,
    Near Guernsey's silver sands.

A blue rift opened in that pall
    With snowy swathings bound,
As 'neath the ancient city wall
    Our swift course onward wound;
Bright rays of light on vale and stream,
    While forth, through tears of rain,
York's minster towers and steeples gleam,
    And Holy Mary's fane.

On a low white couch, laid to her rest,
    Is a silent breathless form;
With small hands folded on her breast,
    In the hush'd air, soft and warm.
Set free from pain, and earth's embrace,
    In pure white robes arrayed;
With dim light falling on her face,
    Pale roses round her laid.

She could not speak to call me home –
    No voice, no sound was there—
No wildly-weeping friends had come,
    Gathered as mourners near;

But one knelt low on bended knee,
    And with perpetual moan,
My sister's voice had summoned me
    To share that vigil lone.

R. M. K.

THE SISTER'S GRAVE.

The thunder-clouds hung over us,
   The day, though sad, was still,
When we followed close behind thy bier,
   On Malvern's wooded hill:
While softly on our drooping heads,
   From the lowering skies above,
Like angels' tears, large drops fell down -
   The summer rain of love.

As our footsteps lingered,
   On their painful, weary way,
I saw thee pressing onward,
   I heard thee lightly say—
"Come faster, sisters, join me—
   Come to the vantage ground;
Leave clouds and mists behind you,
   Here all is light around!

"Below, in earth's deep valleys,
   I have fought a weary strife;
There, pain and grief and sadness
   Have worn away my life.
Here fresher breezes fan me,
   Cool shadows round me spread,
And gushing founts and pearly dews
   New life have o'er me shed."

Lightly her form passed onwards,
Firmly the small feet trod
   A path that, up the steep hillside,
Seemed lifting her to God.

With buoyant step she moved along,
While her slight fingers clasped
    The travellers' joy and ivy wreaths ,
That o'er the heights were cast.

I thought of days, long past and gone,
    Whilst that slow procession moved,
When the prostrate form before us borne
    Had been our best beloved!
When foremost in the rugged path,
    First on the steep hillside,
That slender shape, with airy grace,
    Before us used to glide.

Then—sadly home returning –
    We see thy vacant place;
While the green hills fold around thee,
    Like a mother's fond embrace.
Beneath the sheltering yew-trees,
    Under the smooth green sod,
We have laid her gently to her rest—
    The perfect rest of God!

                                        R. M. K.

COMMENTARY
by
Alan McKenzie

I was asked by Alex (Sandy) Mackenzie in Dundee, Scotland to republish his very rare book, *The Last Mackenzie of Redcastle* by Rosa Mackenzie Kettle.

There were a number of questions we needed to answer before committing ourselves to the re-publication of this book. Rosa Mackenzie Kettle was a somewhat popular author of romantic novels in the late 19th century and she wrote in a style that today seems dated. She inserts many poems in the book some of which are written by herself, and others by more famous poets.

Rosa states that she is the granddaughter of the last Mackenzie of Redcastle and describes some of his possessions she still has in her keeping, including his seal and a valuable diamond ring.

The first hint that the facts she presents may not be entirely accurate appears at the start of Chapter One, where she states: "Nor do I consider myself bound to adhere strictly to the truth in this romantic chronicle. Those circumstances which affect the principal characters are essentially true. In other cases names and dates have been purposely altered to prevent annoyance or misconstruction."

In the next paragraph she writes: "Many years have elapsed since that far away time; so there is little cause to fear that this story of our grandfather will give pain to any mortal living, while the facts on which it is founded are well worth recording."

There are a number of historical reports on Rosa's grandfather which puts him in a very poor light but that portion of his life appears nowhere in her book. Throughout the book, which is written in the form of a romantic novel, the hero, George Mackenzie, is presented as an upright, popular soldier and a true gentleman of that era. But since the story comes to an end while he is still a young man we have to ask ourselves if Rosa was fully aware of the dreadful reputation attached to her grandfather.

What do we know of Rosa? She was born in England around 1818 as Mary Rosa Stuart Kettle, and she adopted the maiden name of her mother, Hannah Mackenzie, as her *nom-de-plume*. She was a spinster and she died in March 1895 in Callander where she lived with her sister, Clara. The book was published in 1888 when she was about 70 years of age.

Despite the fact that many used copies of Rosa's other books can be easily found, *The Last Mackenzie of Redcastle* is a rare edition that appears to have been privately published

Was she aware of the bad name her grandfather had?

Let us look at some of the facts concerning the last few Mackenzies of Redcastle. The obvious starting point is Alexander Mackenzie's *History of the Mackenzies with Genealogies of the Principal Families of that Name,* first published in 1879. It contains basic information on the later Redcastle family members, and surely she must have known about it. The following is a brief summary of the family tree in Alexander Mackenzie's volume:

Roderick Mackenzie, sixth of Redcastle, usually called "Ruairi Mor" who married first to Margaret Calder by whom he had seven sons and a daughter. He also had 12 other sons and two daughters of whom little is known. His heir after his death in 1751 was:

Roderick Mackenzie, seventh of Redcastle, known as "Ruairi Bàn". He married in 1730, Hannah Anna Murdoch of Cambodden, Galloway with issue:
1. Kenneth, his heir and successor.
2. Captain John (who succeeded as VI of Kincraig.)
3. Alexander—died in infancy.
4. Roderick—died in infancy.
5. Margaret, who on 29th November, 1755 married Sir Alexander Mackenzie, Tenth of Gairloch. She died 1759, with issue.
6. Mary, born 1732, died unmarried at age 96.
7. Elizabeth born 1746, married Aug. 1782 Major-General Colin Mackenzie, with issue.

8. Christina, born 1749.
9. Jean born 1752 married Robert Anderson, Glasgow, died 1819, without issue.

Roderick's wife died at Redcastle 1755 at age of 39. Roderick died at Inverness on 10th May, 1785.

Note here that Kenneth's mother died when he was around 9 years old and that suggests Rosa's history here may be correct. But there is no mention of the second wife of "Muckle Colin" that George despised. It is not unreasonable that the "Laird" would have married again as he survived for 30 years after his wife's death.

Captain Kenneth Mackenzie, eighth of Redcastle, Born 21 February 1748, married at Edinburgh on 17th August, 1767, Jean, daughter of James Thomson, Accountant-General of Excise in Scotland, with issue—
1. Roderick, his heir and successor
2. Hector, who married in Edinburgh on 29th of March, 1800, Diana Davidson, daughter of Dr. Davidson of the H.E.I.C.S. (Honourable East India Company's Service.) with issue.
3. Boyd, who married William MacCall of Newton-Stewart, without issue.
4. Hanna, the last surviving child of Kenneth of Redcastle, married William MacCa, of Barnshalloch, and died at Creebridge, Newton-Stewart, on 8th

Captain Kenneth Mackenzie of Redcastle - portrait by Kay

of August, 1849, age 83 years.

Captain Kenneth was tried for the murder of Kenneth Mackenzie, alias Jefferson. He was found guilty and sentenced to be hanged, but afterwards pardoned. He divorced his wife; went abroad; entered the Russian service; and was killed in 1789 near Constantinople, where he was Assistant Consul, in a duel with Captain Smith, master of a merchant ship, to whom he had entrusted all his property when he had got into trouble about Jefferson. He figures in *John Kay's - Original Portraits* as one of the Bucks of the City.

He was succeeded by his eldest son,

Roderick Mackenzie, ninth of Redcastle. He never took possession. The estate being encumbered, he sold it in June, 1790, to James Grant of Corriemony, for £25,450, whose nephew, Patrick Grant, sold it in 1828 to Sir William Fettes of Comely Bank, Bart., for £135,000.

. .

This Roderick, the last direct male representative of the House of Redcastle, died in 1798, in Jamaica, unmarried, when the representation of the family devolved upon his uncle, Captain John Mackenzie, VI. of Kincraig.

The first problem is to identify which person is the "Last Mackenzie of Redcastle" named "George Mackenzie" in Rosa's book. If it is Roderick 9th of Redcastle the problem is that he died in Jamaica, unmarried and probably aged around 29. Since Rosa is supposed to have used Mackenzie as her nom de plume after her mother and since her mother was said to be Hanna Mackenzie, then her grandfather would have been Captain Kenneth Mackenzie, 8th of Redcastle. In any event both Kenneth and his son Roderick died in 1789 and 1798 respectively and Rosa was not born until around 1818. Thus she had no personal knowledge of her grandfather and given his reputation it is possible that Rosa was fed some stories to put her grandfather in a more favourable light.

Reference is made in Alexander Mackenzie's *History of the Mackenzies* that Kenneth Mackenzie is featured in Kay's Edinburgh Portraits as one of the four bucks of the city.

Kay used to walk about the city and he would draw a picture of any person he thought was interesting and in this way he persuaded Kenneth to have his portrait included in one of his volumes (there are four volumes). Included, quite aside from the portrait shown, is a lengthy write-up which reports as follows:

> The third figure in the print is an excellent likeness of the somewhat notorious CAPTAIN M'KENZIE of Red Castle. . . .
> This gentleman was an officer in the Seaforth's Regiment of Highlanders, at the time of their revolt in 1778.

This famous revolt by the Seaforth Highlanders was well dealt with in John Prebble's book *Mutiny*, and records how officers and men declared that neither their bounty nor their arrears of pay had been fully paid up and that they had otherwise been ill-used.

> Kay relates an anecdote of Captain M'Kenzie during the mutiny, highly characteristic of his fortitude and determined disposition. One day while he was in command over the Canongate Jail, where a few of the mutineers were confined,

Redcastle in happier times

Redcastle came into the ownership of the Baillies of Dochfour, in whose absentee ownership the roof slates were removed in the 1950s - leading to the castle's speedy dereliction and present lamentable condition.

a party from Arthur Seat came to demand their liberation. The Captain sternly refused—the soldiers threatened to take his life, and pointed their bayonets at him; but he bared his breast, and telling them to strike, at the same time declared that not a single man should be liberated. The effect of this resolute conduct was instantaneous—the men recovered arms, and retired to their encampment.

Prebble puts a different light on what happened by saying that the men ironically cheered his courage, threw him down the steps and opened the door, releasing the prisoners. In another part of *Mutiny* Prebble states that Kenneth was a hot-tempered and purse-poor bravo, he considered himself an invincible duellist and within a week of joining the regiment he fought three contests with its officers. He would have engaged in a fourth some months later, declaring his dignity outraged by a mustard-pot hurled across the mess table, had not his weary colleagues demanded his court-martial.

Kay proceeds:

Captain M'Kenzie afterwards incurred an unfortunate celebrity from a circumstance which reflected less credit upon him than the above act of heroism, and for which abuse of power he was tried at the Old Bailey, London, on the 11th December, 1784.

He had been sent out in 1782, as captain of an independent company, to act against the Dutch on the coast of Africa; and was there appointed to the command of a small fortification, called Fort Morea. Among the prisoners of the fort was a person of the name of Murray Kenneth M'Kenzie alias Jefferson, who had been confined for desertion. (He had deserted twice previously. He had been heard to express his resolution of murdering M'Kenzie, and had, moreover, endeavoured to induce soldiers to mutiny). Jefferson, possessing more than common address, prevailed on the sentry to let him escape; upon learning which, Captain M'Kenzie was in a violent passion. He caused the sentinel to be punished with more than fifteen hundred lashes, and immediately despatched a party of soldiers in search of the runaway. The men returned, however, without success; upon which he ordered the guns to be charged and directed against a small village in the neighbourhood, named Black Town, where he supposed the prisoner had taken refuge, and he gave notice that, if Jefferson was not instantly delivered up, he would blow the town to atoms. A shot or two had the desired effect. About three thousand natives were seen approaching the fort, with Jefferson in the centre. No sooner had the prisoner been brought into court than the Captain gave him to understand that he had not a moment to live. Then ordering one of the cannons to be prepared, had him instantly lashed to the muzzle of the piece. The prisoner bade one of his comrades beg for one half hour to say his prayers; but the answer the Captain returned was—"No, you rascal; if any man speaks a word in his favour I will blow out his brains;" at the same time brandishing his pistol which he held in his hand. A portion of the burial-service being read to the prisoner, the Captain ordered the prayer-book to be pulled out of his hands. Jefferson then hastily took leave of his comrades; and, after upbraiding the tyrant, as he called the Captain, gave the signal. In a moment the match was applied, and the next the prisoner was blown over the wall. His remains were afterwards picked up by the men and interred.

In defence of such an extraordinary and savage stretch of power, Captain M'Kenzie endeavoured to prove that his company were mutinous—that Jefferson had been a ringleader, and had been repeatedly heard to threaten the life of the Captain. The evidence was by no means conclusive as to this allegation; and the shocking sentence does not strengthen his assertion. It appeared, however, from unquestionable authority, that he had a very worthless set of characters under his command—the garrison being mostly composed of convicts; and besides, he had not the means of forming a court-martial for the trial of the prisoner.

The jury found M'Kenzie guilty of wilful murder; but, in consideration of the "desperate crew he had to command," they recommended him to mercy. During the trial and passing of sentence, the Captain behaved with the utmost composure. His execution was first delayed for a week—then he was respited—and ultimately pardoned.

After obtaining his liberty, the captain returned to his native country; and during his stay in Edinburgh, afforded Kay an opportunity of taking his likeness as one of "The Bucks." On observing the Print in the booksellers' windows, The Captain was offended at being classed, as he said, "with fiddlers and madmen." He called on the artist and offered a guinea to have it altered; but, finding his entreaty vain, he insisted on leaving half-a-guinea, for which he soon after got a miniature painting of himself.

Although M'Kenzie had incapacitated himself for the British service, yet being still "intent on war," he resolved to try his hand against the Turks. With this view he entered the ranks of the Russian army, and served in the war against the Turks. He was at last killed in a duel with a fellow-officer, not far from Constantinople.

If Rosa has produced a book about her grandfather

who bears little of the personality of her supposedly real grandfather, Kenneth Mackenzie, we could draw a line and just say that she was spun some tale about her grandfather which kept her in the dark because of the name and repute of the Mackenzies of Redcastle. But before we do that how accurate is the story told by Kay (published in 1842!) and repeated by Alexander Mackenzie?

Consider, then, another history of the same family which, while still holding Kenneth in bad repute, nevertheless it is totally different from Kay's tale!

This version was published in Dingwall in 1848 and is entitled, *Historical and Traditional Sketches of Highland Families and of the Highlands* by John Maclean. He writes an interesting story about the various Mackenzie Lairds of Redcastle, who were at one time a very prosperous family. It gets interesting when he reaches the story of the last Laird of Redcastle since the writer claims to have known him:

> The last Laird of Redcastle of the name of Mackenzie, was Collector of Customs at Inverness and was well known to the narrator. He was a most amiable man, condescending in his manners, and arduous in the duties of his office, which he discharged satisfactorily for a considerable time, but from the circumstances of his eldest son Kenneth joining himself with a band of determined smugglers, the good old gentleman was viewed with a jealous eye. Kenneth was not long associated with this lawless band when he had the boldness to bring them with him to his father's Castle of Redcastle, and there, for safety, deposited their contraband goods.

The worthy Laird his father, who was residing at his post in Inverness, was not till then aware of the illegal and evil career his son was pursuing, although at the same time his hopes were far from sanguine regarding him, as from his youth upwards he was of an over-rambling disposition. However, there was now no alternative for Collector Mackenzie, but to resign his situation, a situation he filled with honour and integrity. He was much felt for and sympathised with by both high and low throughout the north, and particularly so by the inhabitants of Inverness. Kenneth seeing what his folly brought his venerable parent to, like the prodigal son, immediately abandoned his iniquitous career. A short time after this he commenced the droving trade—a more lawful occupation—but not being successful, he soon gave it up for the more honourable one of fighting for his king and country, having got a commission in the 78th, or Ross-shire Highlanders. So keen and eager was he in enlistments, that he forced several poor fellows out of their beds on his father's estate, to accompany him to India's shores. This work of compulsion he even had the boldness to carry on in Inverness, where he trepanned not a few, among whom there was one of the name of Gunn, whose mother was a reputed witch, and whose awful imprecations were fearfully levelled against him and his family, for tearing away her only child. Sometime after, while with his regiment in India, he was charged at the instance of the Government with fraud, for which he was called home and confined for the rest of his lifetime in the Tower of London. In the midst of grief and sorrow, his venerable parent calmly and meekly resigned his spirit into the hand of his eternal Father, in whose mansions the cares, toils, and disappointments of this world below are not known. The estate subsequently became much burdened, and as the second son John, who was also in the army, and was much beloved and respected by his brother officers, and every one who had the pleasure of his acquaintance, was not in circumstances to redeem it, it was put up for sale. A wealthy scion of the clan offered largely for it, and the only impediment in the way of getting it was his being the son of a tinker, (but he was a good and honest man although horn spoon-making, &c., was his calling.) It was, however, purchased by the Grants, then by Sir William Fettes, and after his death by the present proprietor, Col. Baillie of Tarradale, the Lord-Lieutenant of the county.

Here we have a yet different story of the subject of our review—Captain Kenneth Mackenzie, 8th of Redcastle. We only have the reports of the few people who knew the family in the 18th century and we all know how difficult it is to prove a genealogy unless there are written records to prove the family tree.

We may well feel inclined to disbelieve the history as written by his granddaughter Rosa, but there is no other record available which deals with the family's adventures in America during the War of Independence, and particularly the interesting record of their association with the prestigious Portuguese family at their house of Casa Bianca in the United States and of their lives in Lisbon at the time of the big earthquake and tsunami which laid waste to the city in 1755. We have little knowledge at all of Rosa's family except from this book, where we are allowed to get quite confused through the renaming of the real people and changing of the dates of their lives "to protect the innocent" as we say in the modern world.

So, we are inclined to re-publish this book after a lapse of 127 years. We leave it to the reader to draw his or her own conclusions as to the veracity of Rosa's history, written in the form of a romantic novel of the 19th century.

In *Redcastle–A Place in Scotland's History*, by Dr Graham Clark, (Athena Press, London 2009) there are further details of the author's findings concerning Captain Kenneth Mackenzie of Redcastle.

Alan McKenzie, FSA Scot.,
Lieutenant to Cabarfeidh,
Clan MacKenzie Society of Canada